I0702549

THIS IS LIFE

REDISCOVERED SHORT FICTION
BY FRANK LONDON BROWN

FOREWORD BY DEBRA E. BROWN-THOMPSON
FOREWORD BY REBECCA ZORACH
INTRODUCTION BY SANDRA JACKSON-OPOKU
AFTERWORD BY NILE LANSANA
EDITED BY MICHAEL W. PHILLIPS JR.

Publication of this book supported in part by a grant from the Department of Art History at Northwestern University.

Print book design and layout by Michael W. Phillips Jr.
Ebook design and layout by Carson Winter

Published by From Beyond Press | Chicago, IL
frombeyondpress.com
mike@frombeyondpress
Instagram & Twitter: @frombeyondpress

ISBN: 979-8-9875743-2-4

Library of Congress Control Number: 2023937768

CONTENTS

FOREWORD

BEARING WITNESS TO THE RICH BLACK EXPERIENCE
BY DEBRA E. BROWN-THOMPSON

"Girl, do that homework!"

That's the way my father, Frank London Brown, began his letter to me. He had written four letters, one each to my sisters, my mother, and me. They were given to my mother after his funeral by our family friend, Gwendolyn Brooks, whom he had entrusted with them until after his death.

So, I did. I did my homework. I read with immense pride, compassion, and a few tears, this newly discovered treasure of short stories written by my father for the *Chicago Daily Defender*.

I am struck by the powerful impact these stories had on me. His innate ability to capture micro-expressions of people and micro-moments of time that pierce, resonate, and dwell in the depths of our hearts and souls is uncanny. These captivating stories delve so deeply inside some aspects of Black life that many Black people themselves have not dared to explore them.

As one might imagine, reading these vignettes brought back a flood of memories. The distinct clatter of his typewriter keys on Sunday mornings with Thelonious Monk or Charlie "Bird" Parker echoing through the house is as clear as day. Daddy would sit there, typing away on his black typewriter, illuminated by a classic banker's lamp with a brass stand and green glass lampshade. He would lean in toward the typed pages rolling up from the machine and sport a faint smile of satisfaction with his ability to magically turn mere words into almost tangible images.

My father had a remarkable ability to bring to life the qualities he perceived in others as he created composites of people who journeyed into his life. As a spouse, father, journalist, machinist, musician, and civil rights activist, his life experiences lent credibility to his range of actors from the insanely in love to those apathetic about human life. As an English literature educator, I realized how his writing reflected his own growth as an author. As his daughter, I understand how his works provided insight into the richness of Black culture.

While these vignettes are easy to read, they are riddled with complex relationships, social commentary, and moral dilemmas. These stories display a gift of creative range from a coming-of-age tone as in "Really Clean":

For the first time in her life, she put on not only cologne, but bath water, some of her father's after-shave lotion, and deodorant, all in small quantities to be sure, and lastly, on went a dash of lipstick!

to a heavier tone of death as in "The Riddle."

All of his works, however, exude hope and an unwavering determination to optimize life's brief timeline, as in "Just People" where he reminds us that life always has the potential for joy.

One story, "Love III," really struck me, and I laughed as he so aptly described the men at Fifty-Eighth and Calumet. There was a candy store near that corner in the basement of a brownstone. Whenever Mommy gave us money, we would run to buy Mary Janes and dill pickles, passing right by the two men he so vividly describes. I can see them now elbowing each other as we ran by, saying:

"De Thomas, these youngsters these days are smart as whippersnappers. You hear what that mannish little thing said just now?"
"I heard him, Wilson. It's all this TV and jet planes and . . ."
". . . no God in their lives. That's the main thing."

Undoubtedly, the reader will also find a personal connection. Some stories are serious and thought-provoking, while others are lighthearted and amusing. Some are academic and brainy, while others are streetwise. Yet, all are unafraid to explore uncomfortable truths, often revealing secrets we would prefer to keep private, as in the rather humorous "Homer, Your Turn."

Through this collection, my father invites readers to peek through the windows of 133 lives. As voyeurs, we are compelled to bear witness to their stories, joys, sorrows, and complexities so eloquently wrapped in the essence of the Black experience with empathy, insight, and authenticity.

Enjoy the journeys of these stories through life's preciously short timelines, just as my father did when he wrote them.

FOREWORD

IMAGES OF BLACK CHICAGO
BY REBECCA ZORACH

The cover photo of this book was taken by Robert Abbott "Bobby" Sengstacke Jr. (1943–2017), a talented and prolific photographer who created thousands of images of Black Chicago in the twentieth century and beyond. The great-nephew of Robert Sengstacke Abbott, the founder of the *Chicago Defender,* Sengstacke worked for the *Defender* and for the Nation of Islam newspaper *Muhammad Speaks* as a photojournalist. His photographs of Black celebrities and political figures have appeared widely in numerous publications and films.

Sengstacke contributed photographs to the Wall of Respect, a pathbreaking public mural in the Bronzeville neighborhood, and documented the mural and its community exhaustively. He created and contributed to other South Side murals that combined painting and photography. He worked closely with artists and helped found the annual art exhibition *Black Esthetics*—now called *Black Creativity*—at the Museum of Science and Industry. His images of the Black Arts Movement offer unparalleled views of important and otherwise little-seen artists, musicians, and events. And just like Frank London Brown's short short fiction, Sengstacke's portraits of ordinary Chicagoans enjoying the Bud Billiken parade, the Wall of Respect, or a concert at Cabrini Green afford insights into the lives of regular people in mid-twentieth century Black Chicago.

He also helped make this book possible. I had the opportunity to work with Bobby Sengstacke in the last decade of his life to organize parts of his vast archive and scan thousands of his negatives to help make them available online. I was also working on a book on the Black Arts Movement, *Art for People's Sake,* and got to ask him many questions about the personalities involved in the images and stories he chronicled. He had stories about the celebrated artists of the Wall of Respect and AFRICOBRA, and about the community members who collaborated in their projects. His insights were an immense gift to my book.

As I pieced together an understanding of the story of the Black Arts Movement in Chicago, I interviewed other people, too. Gerald Williams, a founding member of AFRICOBRA, told me a story about how the characteristic lettering, so prominent in AFRICOBRA artworks, came to be:

> I can recall as clear as day, riding the L on the way to school, and as late as 1960, or as early as 1960, the words "Bird Lives." On a wall, facing the El station at about 43rd street, probably like 39th, before you get to 35th. But in big letters, BIRD LIVES, and it stayed on that building for, oh, a long time, probably until the '70s, mid-'70s. But that kind of lettering, or expression, was common, and so we pulled that into what would be an important principle to incorporate into our work, a living statement about something that's going on.[1]

It was a compelling story of graffiti sparking something in these artists' practice before graffiti was considered an art form in itself. I wondered if I might find something about a BIRD LIVES graffito—better known for its New York circulation, originated by the jazz poet and painter Ted Joans—near a Chicago L station. So I searched the digitized articles of the *Chicago Defender*, and found "Bird Lives," a short short story about a sad man whose dreams soar to the sounds of Charlie Parker, and who, after Parker's death, scratches these words on a wall with a soft brick. It was signed only with a mysterious "F. L. B."

Knowing Bobby's history with the *Defender*, I asked him who F. L. B. might be. He paused, suggested someone else from the newspaper whom I could ask. Then a lightbulb went on: "Frank London Brown."

I was intrigued; it was Mike Phillips's idea to make a comprehensive search for Brown's texts, and it took his tenacity to bring them to publication. But like many things, this collection could never have existed without Bobby's contribution.

---

1. https://never-the-same.org/interviews/gerald-williams/

EDITOR'S NOTE

BY MICHAEL W. PHILLIPS JR.

These stories appeared in the *Chicago Daily Defender* between November 2, 1959 and November 3, 1960. They appear here in order of earliest publication date. Some of them also appeared later in the national edition of the paper.

I have refrained from editing the stories, with a few exceptions:

- numbered streets have been standardized (e.g., Fifty-Fifth Street)
- obvious misspellings have been corrected
- in rare cases, I have corrected details in the stories, but only when they were obvious mistakes. In each case, I have included a footnote explaining the change.

I have included footnotes to provide context where I deemed them appropriate.

INTRODUCTION

ONE HUNDRED THIRTY-THREE SAXOPHONE SOLOS
BY SANDRA JACKSON-OPOKU

I knew him briefly in the mid-1950s, a "knowing" precluded by the fact that Frank London Brown was a grown man with a wife and family, and I was a three-year-old child who hadn't started school yet.

Yet of all the adults who passed through my childhood, Frank London Brown made a distinct impression. He worked in a factory like other Black fathers, but he was a writer too. A real live writer! This made him famous in our eyes. Then too, our small community lived through, and bonded over, a traumatic period in Chicago history. I've heard those events referred to as race riots, though what happened in Trumbull Park was unvarnished White terrorism.

When we consider today's derelict state of public housing, it's difficult to imagine that these dwellings once represented efforts at mid-20th-century progress. Housing projects were a flawed, ambitious experiment in urbanism that appeared to offer poor families a leg up. The original residents of many public housing developments, in fact, were working-class White folks.

Trumbull Park was a community of squat, two-story rowhouses and three-story apartment buildings on the city's far southeastern edge, butting up against the Indiana border. Though built right before World War II, the place seemed fresh and promising, from its sprawling, manicured grounds, brick-fronted buildings, gleaming white fixtures, and modern appliances.

Yet no welcome wagon met the Browns, the Jacksons, or any of the other Negro families that began arriving in 1953. Instead of cookie platters, we were met with fury and flames. Bricks crashed through our windows, incendiary devices thrown in after them. Fires were set ablaze that not only burned out some Black families, but adjacent White neighbors as well. "Cutting off your nose to spite your face" seemed an appropriate motto for those moments.

Black men and women were subject to regular acts of verbal abuse and physical assault. Racial slurs were hurled at Black children when we ventured outside to play. Over six decades later, I can still hear my mother's screams when someone pushed a live snake through our front door mail slot. I still remember the sight of it slithering across the floor.

I suspect the only thing preventing a full-on bloodbath was the round-the-clock detail of armed peace officers. Mind you, Chicago police at the time had no great love for its Black citizenry. *Time Magazine* had already done a story in 1954 on the "race riots." It just wouldn't do to sanction a massacre of Negroes in government-supported housing.

Frank London Brown would later chronicle these events in the semi-autobiographical novel *Trumbull Park*, published to critical acclaim in 1959. Although he described them as very light skinned, his characterization of one Trumbull Park family seemed otherwise like my own: a pretty young mother of two preschoolers, a boy and a girl. A handsome, temperamental father over-fond of his liquor and struggling to hold down a job. My mother went to her grave convinced that "Frank London Brown wrote that book about me."

The example that Brown represented as a working writer had a deep effect on me, pre-literate though I was. I went around the house finding stray books. I would draw and scribble in the margins and flyleaves, convinced that I, too was "writing books."

When Frank London Brown died tragically at 34, he was publishing in national journals, magazines, and newspapers. His second novel, *The Myth Maker,* was released posthumously in 1969. Though I freelanced for the *Chicago Defender* in the 1970s, I was unaware that Brown had actually written a series of stories that ran from 1959 to 1960 in the storied Black newspaper.

Today this rediscovered trove of 133 works might well be defined as flash fiction. These collected short-short stories, condensed essays, and philosophical meditations place Brown in the tradition of previous *Defender* writers. Langston Hughes's "everyman" narrator, Jess B. Semple, made pithy observations on working-class Black life, while Lou Downey penned gossipy, humorous slice-of-life pieces under the *nom de guerre* "Charlie Cherokee."

In *This Is Life,* Frank London Brown throws opens the windows of midcentury urban Black experience. People listen to records on their hi-fis. Television is replacing radio as the broadcast medium of choice. Blood is in the air, courtesy of the recent Korean War and the murder of Emmett Till. Ghana becomes independent while anticolonial movements rage through Africa and across the globe. Here on American soil, the modern Civil Rights Movement is born, while the Great Migration from the South has been steadily darkening the urban Northlands.

I ain't shamed to say I'm from Miss. Sippi. A white man didn't think about callin' me out of my name. That's why I'm up here right today.

Yet some moments seem remarkably contemporary: an epidemic of street violence, the aimlessness of urban youth, drug addiction, mental illness, and systemic racism. There are vivid encounters between Black people and the criminal justice system: judges, police detectives, and patrol officers. Not all police*men* in these stories are monsters, though many are . . . and all of them are male.

This Is Life will introduce you to unforgettable characters, "winoes, rentmen, swingmen, bosses, foremen, and policemen that floated in and out of his life like dirty corks upon a filthy sea." They cycle through domestic intrigues, workplace melodramas, romantic heart-break and healing, racial bias and retribution. They find themselves in sad comedies of error, pregnant ironies, misapprehensions, and mis-placed masculinities. Some are frozen mannequins of ennui. Others detonate into reckless, random acts of violence.

You may be reminded of Black Chicago literary realists like Gwendolyn Brooks, with her iconic "kitchenette building," or Lorraine Hansberry's *A Raisin in the Sun.* Here poor people in overcrowded rooms can barely afford the children they bear, yet struggle to hold onto dignity.

There are "O. Henry" twists aplenty, stories whose journeys veer off into unexpected destinations. Two buddies seem to be shooting the breeze, waxing philosophical on "the nature of man." Yet we realize it's not the "breeze" they're shooting when the hired guns pause to execute a hit. As one man motors along Lake Shore Drive, the sights and pungent smells of Lake Michigan bring to mind a woman he once loved . . . and murdered.

Some pieces take place in expansive battlefields and streetscapes, others cram themselves into claustrophobic confines of car interiors, parlors, bedrooms, and bars. You will meet the city as a setting and a character, colorful neighborhoods and treacherous street corners, the lakefront and nightclubs . . . 47th Street, Cottage Grove, Madison Avenue, The Strand Hotel, Congress Expressway, South Parkway before it became Martin Luther King Drive. Mentions of DuSable always mean the high school; the now-famous museum of African American history hasn't yet been founded. Many of these landmarks no longer exist, though some are still around.

Chicago-centric though this collection may be, some stories move beyond the city limits, traveling from pre-revolutionary Havana to Korean battlefields, Mexico to Mississippi. We even get to eavesdrop on the Mau Mau Rebellion in British Colonial East Africa and witness a presciently dystopian Hawai'ian landscape in the throes of a global pandemic.

Love is explored in various permutations: romantic, marital and extramarital, obsessive, transactional, parental love (and its absence), lost, and unrequited. One man even falls in love with a ghost he dubs "Baby-Sweets." Or, consider the throbbing heartache of "No 'Forever.'"

What is there to say when your lover is gone and the hole she left is left wringing in the singing and the ringing wind? Or when she has left there at its bottom (the hole's) a tiny quivering thing or nothing that beats and hurts and burns till her absence is like her presence and her presence is like her absence?

Frank London Brown's own eclectic work life included stints as a vocalist and writings on jazz artists. Music and musicians define the theme and style, the characters on these pages. Ornette Coleman, Frank Sinatra, Nat King Cole, Joe Williams, Thelonious Monk, and Charlie "Bird" Parker provide the soundtrack. In "The Benediction":

It started with an alto horn, and a young boy who'd grown faster than he should have, and who'd become great before he should have, and who sought for the source of the feeling deep inside before he should have . . . All this strained inside him, strained and drove him, pushed him and made him whip his fingers upon the valves of his horn until they hurt.

In another scene, Black musicians marvel at a White horn player's deep evocation of the blues idiom.

The sax-man nearest him turned to the other and laughed silently. Where, he thought, did this cat get our sadness, our misery, the secret of the drive, and tears in our horns?

When the set ends and musicians leave the stage . . .

They passed a dark woman whose stomach spoke of child. Someone pushed by them and to the woman, saying in a low worried voice,
"Honey, what are you doing here? How'd you get here? Have you eaten?"
The sax-men turned to see. It was the guy who had blown so much soul; so much anger, love, tears and great happiness through his horn . . . Silent answer to their questioning looks.

This man had come to the blues not through racial inheritance, but for the love of his pregnant wife and the struggles she's endured.
From existential soliloquys, to meditations on unfulfilled experience, to the healing balm of laughter, this collection is life writ large by a man who lived it fully, if not for very long.

And now you see that heaven was where you were, my man. And now you see that sleep is a long thing, a lonesome trip with no passing trees or poles to mark off minutes or centuries . . .

One hundred thirty-three saxophone solos riff across these pages. Welcome in. The music awaits you.

THIS IS LIFE

BY FRANK LONDON BROWN

SILENT ANSWER
NOVEMBER 2, 1959

The lights around the bandstand drew him out like a boll of white cotton on the dry brown ground. His straight hair seemed out of place as he stood alongside the two dark, crinkle-haired sax-men.

It was a jam session. The two dark men had finished their solos—bristling with bursts of notes, and longstanding anger. Now it was the white man's turn. Putting his sax to his mouth, he blew; shoulders hunched, eyes closed, frowning, matching sad note for sad note with the Negroes, and glad note for glad note, soaring in the vapor trails they made, recalling Bird, John Gilmore, Sonny Rollins—all the sad ones, all the extra glad ones.

The sax-man nearest him turned to the other and laughed silently. Where, he thought, did this cat get our sadness, our misery, the secret of the drive, and tears in our horns?

The set ended. The Negroes shook the white man's hand, and walked toward a table. They passed a dark woman whose stomach spoke of child. Someone pushed by them and to the woman, saying in a low worried voice,

"Honey, what are you doing here? How'd you get here? Have you eaten?"

The sax-men turned to see. It was the guy who had blown so much soul; so much anger, love, tears and great happiness through his horn . . . Silent answer to their questioning looks.

DADDYS DO LIE
NOVEMBER 3, 1959

"Daddy, a nice man gave me a nickel."

"Oh? When?"

"Last night."

"What was the man's name?"

"I can't tell you. Mommy asked not to."

"Oh, come on. I won't tell anybody."

"You won't tell Mommy I told you? 'Cause she wouldn't never tell me any more secrets if you told her I told you. Honest, you won't tell, Daddy?"

The Daddy picked his son up, and hugged him, and kissed his cheek.

"I promise; now who was the man?"

"He was George."

"George Roberts?"

"Uh, huh. And he's real nice."

That night the little boy lay in his bed, and angry voices grew louder and louder through the wall between his room and his mother and father's.

"You're a lie! I know he was here. Bucky told me!"

The boy sat up in his bed. Fear had him, but more than that the cold pain of his first betrayal twisted around and around in him. He had not known before that grownups . . . daddys could tell lies.

HOMER, YOUR TURN
NOVEMBER 4, 1959

He had not expected anything like this to happen. For the first time, the light that touched her face brought out the brown in a rash of colors that were more than brown.

The reds, yellows, and even purple specks of her skin seemed to light up by themselves, and the lines in her lips as she smiled and talked and moved before him seemed to become apparent for the first time too. Her perfume filled his nose and he swallowed it, and breathed deeply as she passed him again.

Suddenly he became ashamed, and began to feel as though someone might have seen his face, and learned his thoughts. He swallowed and looked downward, and jumped when she spoke to him.

"Homer, will you come to the board and do the next geometry problem?"

JUST DON'T KNOW
NOVEMBER 5, 1959

The squad cars screeched around the block like burning women. Lang stopped running. Mumbling to himself and crying, and gasping to breathe. He pointed the gun in the direction of the lights that moved on him, flashing red, and white, and emitting high sighing whines, that split the rainy black of the night with tremors of death and danger.

"Hold it, you!" Lang fired. The answering flame staggered him, toppled him and jerked his body about as it huddled, knees doubled on the reddening cement beneath him.

When the officers searched his riddled pants and shirt, they found them empty except for a smeared picture of a man, a taut rope and a leafless tree.

"Why do you suppose he shot O'Leary?" One of the cops said. "All O'Leary did was ask 'im for his driver's license."

The policeman's partner squinted at the wrinkled photograph, made out the situation, gulped, dropped the picture in a nearby waste can, and replied,

"Cheez, I don't know why he woulda done a thing like that."

IDEA BACKFIRES
NOVEMBER 9, 1959

The word went through the plant in ten seconds flat. SOMEBODY'S GONNA GET FIRED TODAY!

Mamie heard it in the ladies' washroom. Having had nothing but bad luck all her natural life, she immediately grew afraid and started trying to figure out something that would assure her own job.

The "something" came at noon. One of the women on her sewing line said,

"What I think we need around here is a union."

Mamie smiled, drank her coffee down, and slid away from the table in the tavern-lunch room across the street from the factory. She walked slowly until she thought she was out of the sight of the other women. Then she broke for the front office, knocked on the door, rehearsed in her mind exactly how she would tell her boss that Ima Jean was talking union talk when the door opened. The boss stepped out. Mamie blurted:

"Uh Mr. Berg, I just heard the girls . . ."

Mr. Berg interrupted her.

"Oh, I'm sorry you had to hear it from them, Mamie, but that's the way it is. I'll give you good references though. You can pick up your check from the timekeeper."

MAÑANA, MAYBE?
NOVEMBER 11, 1959

The blue water from the Bay had turned black as night came to Havana. The woman before James was blonde. She spoke Spanish softly, looking into James's eyes as she spoke. His DuSable[1] Spanish came back to him slowly. He tried to look sophisticated while he desperately rambled back and forth in his mind for the meaning of those lessons which the DuSable Spanish teacher had tried with equal desperation to place there.

But only usted, amigo, and dias came to mind.

"Comprende?"

The words casa, amor, esta noche were as familiar to him as well, as mach, schnell, and achtung, which weren't familiar at all. James smiled and look a long swallow of rum.

"Oh yeah, yo comprende."

"Cuando, ahora?"

---

1. DuSable High School (Brown's alma mater) was located at 49th and Wabash. At its peak in the 1950s, it had a nationally recognized music program led by Walter Dyett and more than 4,000 students. After the demolition of the Robert Taylor Homes surrounding it, enrollment declined and it was closed in 2003. The building currently houses two smaller Chicago Public Schools, the Bronzeville Scholastic Institute and the Daniel Hale Williams School of Medicine.

In absolute desperation, James blurted,

"Mañana."

The woman, flushed, and stared at the table.

Having put herself in the embarrassing position of asking him to visit her apartment, she was hurt by his suggestion that it be put off until morning.

She got up, smiled, touched his hand and spoke the only English she knew.

"Sorry..."

As she left the coffee shop tucked in the unending row of grey buildings along the marble streets of El Prado, Havana's main street, James slapped his knee and mumbled,

"How did I know I'd need to know the ( ) & * - , ?: language!"

MISSING TIE
NOVEMBER 12, 1959

John Thomas was angry. His good tie was nowhere to be found. The meeting was half an hour away, and his house was forty minutes away from the meeting hall. His wife was frantic. His daughter was sitting quietly at the kitchen table poring over her homework; his son followed his footsteps, temerously, holding a paper from which he'd been studying a rather difficult problem in civics.

John brushed by the young, dark, eyeglass-wearing boy. "That tie has to be found!"

"Uh, daddy. Uh. l got a problem, uh...could you look it over? I mean, would you help me?"

John Thomas stopped. He took a deep breath.

"Robert, don't you see me running around here trying to get out of this house to that meeting! I mean, haven't you any consideration for me at all? Are you trying to help me find that tie?"

Robert turned away, looked for and found the tie.

He laid the civics problem on the top of the television set. He turned the fight on. Billy Hunter[2] was doing in Alex Miteff. John Thomas made his meeting. The speaker introduced him.

---

2. Billy Hunter was a Black boxer from Ypsilanti, MI, who defeated Argentine boxer Alex Miteff on September 25, 1959.

"And now ladies and gentlemen, the famous author of *Delinquency and Teenagers Today* . . . Mr. John Thomas!"

Everybody applauded.

THE BROTHERS
NOVEMBER 16, 1959
SHORT, SHORT FEATURE

He had been warned about the neighborhood, but he hadn't believed it. Now he was running. Something inside him over which he had not the slightest control had broken aloose and had filled his legs, and his chest, and his brain with fear; and now he ran. Bricks clumped to the ground around him. Words followed him. Footsteps did. Legs pumping, eyes seeking the cranny into which to dart; he heard the cry. Something in him shut its meaning away from him, but only for short, short seconds.

"They got me, Jerry! Man, they got me! Jerry! Jerry!"

That he had a brother was a fact that was nearly non-existent alongside his desire to live, and not be beaten, stoned, murdered.

But now that fact overrode the desire to live.

YOUR BROTHER!

The footsteps gained, and louder grew the voices at his back. Jerry stopped running, turned, faced the faces that frowned hate at him, glanced but once at the bricks and bats, clenched his fists, and ran . . . toward the men who chased him, toward the sound of his brother's voice.

JUDGMENT DAY
NOVEMBER 17, 1959

The ride along the over-wide, out-arcing boulevard was pleasant. The mist from the gulf coast drifted just above the unnatural blue of Guantanamo Bay, over the sea-pointing tip of land upon which stood the old chiseled features of Havana's greystone Moorish castle.

In front of each car that sped by the castle, across the Prado, down the narrow winds of the Old Section and through the ultra-modern heights of the Havana Hilton, in front of each car, another sped.

Racing endlessly forward with the lead car so far out of sight as to give the feeling of eternity made real, with Oldsmobile chrome, metal, rubber and paint. Eternity racing along the roads which were colored by the un-smoked red of the sun, eternity sinking down into the raw red of earth chopped open to make room for more tall buildings.

One of the soldiers in the Oldsmobile convoy breathed deeply as the smell of thick coffee from an open road fire swept into the car.

"Armando, it is such a nice day. Too nice to do any killing today."

Armando smiled and started to answer, but stopped when the car stopped and the Captain signaled, and the prisoner was brought out of the chalk-white guardhouse, stood along the wall, allowed to pray, glanced once at Armando, and fell, crumpled as Armando and his squad pulled at the metal triggers on their respective rifles.

It had been a nice day.

THE DELAY
NOVEMBER 18, 1959

The plane's wheels touched ground at Miami. The stewardess smiled, and said goodbye in Spanish-tinged English. Clark gripped his grip and gripped, with the other hand, the aluminum railing as he made the steep descent down the ramp.

A friendly southern accent announced when the next planes going to Chicago would be leaving. Clark shuddered as the friendly voice said:

"And dew tew weatha conditions the flat to Chicago will be delayed for three hours. Passanger please pick up your baggage at the other end of the airpote."

Clark started for his seat angry. Three hours!

"Where yuh from man, Chicawgo?"

"Yeah."

"'Havana's something else, ain't it?"

"You KNOW yeah."

"Look," the man's cab-driver badge told Clark that something was happening. "Look, there be a chicken shack down the road apiece. Uh, I don't know what you . . ."

"Like let's go man."

The band had just started playing. A short man was at the mike and he sounded like Ray Charles. A woman smiled at him: she looked like Dorothy Dandridge. Clark mumbled as he danced, "Havana was never like this!"

"Huh!"

"Nothing, honey, nothin'."

"NATURE OF MAN"[3]
NOVEMBER 19, 1959

"It's pretty quiet out here, huh?"

"Yeah, you know, I read a book this morning; a book about man. *What Is the Nature of Man.* That was the name of the book."

"Sounds interesting. What did the book say about man? I mean about the nature of man I mean."

"Well, for one thing, it said that man is, gregar..."

"Gregarious...likes to be around other people."

"That's right. Also, it said that man is really honest, at heart."

"I go along with that. I want something, I'm honest enough to say to myself, 'Like, I want that.' You know?"

"It also said that man is really good, at heart; I mean, like..."

"Hey, wait a minute. Here he comes."

Acting almost as a single man, the two men picked up the shotguns that rested in their laps. A tall man, wearing a white hat and a dark coat, stepped from his car into the dark, tree-shadowed drive in front of a garage. Two blasts stopped him as his hand reached for the button that raised the garage door. He fell without a sound.

A car backed slowly, carefully out of the driveway, moved along the streets, stopped at a stoplight near a corner at which a woman heard a voice say,

"Really, you should read that book; I thought it was swell."

---

3. A handful of stories under the "This Is Life" banner were published without the distinctive "F.L.B." byline, but they were most likely by Brown, judging by their placement and style..

WHEN THEY GOOF
NOVEMBER 21, 1959

"Kill somebody?"

"If they goof, yeah kill 'em. Dig, Jim. This ain't no plaything we gettin' into. I need some bread and I'm gonna get it tonight."

A third young man, sitting on the darkened kitchenette step, who had not spoken before, turned to the first who had spoken and said,

"Like, look Baby, if you chicken, I mean, like forget it. Dig?"

"I ain't scared, I just wanted to know how far you studs are gonna go in this deal."

The second speaker, a tall, muscular youth with an overgrown mustache and a Dizzy Gillespie goatee pointing downward from his lip said,

"Like I said, if they goof they lose." He got up, patted himself, making sure that his butcher knife was secure beneath his belt. It was. He started walking.

"Well, this is it. Let's split."

The other two followed him. The victim was found. He goofed. The butcher knife did its work. The victim died. The "chicken," the "conservative," the cautious one was caught.

Being chicken he confessed to the crime, so as to avoid a beating in the station. Being chicken, he was afraid to implicate the real murderer.

Being chicken, he was fried, was the only one of the three who fried in the electric chair.

COME IN FREE[4]
NOVEMBER 24, 1959

"Last night, night before; twenty-four robbers at my door. I got up, let them in. Hit 'em in the head with a rolling pin. All hid?"

The voice was so far behind Little Junior now that he could hardly hear it. He was scooted far up under the porch. They hadn't ever found him when he hid there and he knew that they wouldn't find him now. The smell of the earth was fresh there, and the dampness was

---

4. Unsigned.

comfortable. Even the dark shadows were comforting. Little Junior lay down and went to sleep.

While he was asleep, footsteps scrambled downstairs and out to the yard. Voices shouted to each other, sirens trilled off-key, brakes screeched, hoses were attached, and water charged from the hoses into the upper floors of the building.

A woman ran through the crowd that surrounded the house crying and calling.

"Little Junior! Little Junior!"

She received no answer.

The fire out, the crowd split and vanished; the firetruck long gone and the first floor tenants working hard to broom-sweep the water from their apartments, Little Junior awakened. He yawned, backed out from under the porch, brushed himself and started back to where, as far as he knew, the kids were still playing.

NOTHING TO DO[5]
NOVEMBER 26, 1959

"So how was work?"

"Okay, honey. More coffee?"

"Yeah, thanks . . . I had a rough day today . . ."

"Really?"

"Yeah. How was your clay?"

"It was alright. Is that coffee hot enough?"

"Yeah. It's hot enough. I guess. the kids are asleep, huh?"

"Yeah, I guess they are. It's ten o'clock."

"Is that all? I thought it was later than that. Anything on TV?"

"No, honey."

"I read the paper already."

"I did too."

"What time did you say it was?"

"Ten."

"I thought it was later than that."

"You said that."

"Yeah, I know I did. Say, what are we waiting up for? Ha, ha. I

5. Unsigned.

mean, there's nothing to do. Huh? Ready to go to bed?"

"May as well. There's nothing else to do."

"Did I ask you how work was today?"

"Yes, you did."

"Oh, well, let's go to bed."

"Okay."

REALLY CLEAN?[6]
DECEMBER 1, 1959

"For the first time in her life, be really clean."

The kids around her locker sang this little ditty whenever Cordella appeared. She had first tried to ignore them, but the singing grew louder and more persistent each time she came to school. Somehow or other, though, this was as far as anyone was willing to go toward informing Cordella of her Very Special Problem.

As inexplicably as birth is (really!), it dawned on the young girl one day. No special reason. No special advice except the "Really Clean" song which she'd not been able to ignore, but which she accepted as her due in life. But just like that, the thought fathered the deed, and indeed Cordelia acted!

For the first time in her life, she put on not only cologne, but bath water, some of her father's after shave lotion, deodorant, all in small quantities lo be sure, and lastly, on went a dash of lipstick! Going to the mirror that morning before school, Cordella brushed her hair, brushed her teeth—twice, and cleaned her fingernails, giving them a lustrous coating of clear polish.

Two boys standing near her locker started their song when Cordella approached.

"For the first time in your . . . uh, your . . . is that you, Cordella?"

Cordella smiled, and spoke in a low, cultured tone she'd never used before:

"Yes, it is I."

In the weeks that followed, Cordella cut down to just a few of the essentials. She felt that something had changed, was different about the entire school, but she was never really sure of what it was.

6. Unsigned.

FAST AND LONG
DECEMBER 2, 1959

The race was fast and the race was long. Billy Cross watched it from a front seat in the Amphitheater. The dark man pulled farther and farther ahead of the white men on the track.

The crowd mumbled as the distance between the Negro and the other runners widened. The distance stretched now to near a quarter of the oval track, and now to nearly half the track, and the crowd began to sense that something was wrong, could not be right, with the way this dark man was running. The mumbles rose to cries, and there was some sound of fear in the cries. Billy Cross stood up. Now the Negro was over three quarters of the track in front of the other runners, gaining now on the last man of the group of runners.

He gained on the last man, caught him, passed him, challenged the leader of the pack for the front place, passed him and while doing so, passed Billy Cross. And Billy cried out at what he saw:

Foam formed on the runner's lips, his eyes were bucked and staring blankly up, muscles bulged from the Negro's neck, cheeks, shoulders; from all of his body. The crowd was screaming; the sound was all fear, now. They too saw that the runner had become something else; was driven now by some urge that was burning him out; that his expression was mixed with agony, and horror, and that he would not stop while he was alive.

X IS THE TIME
DECEMBER 3, 1959

"X is the time I have cried for you, tried to bring you back, but have not and have cried from hurt, undefined, yet coming, I think, from the pain that loss causes me. X? Yes, X for the limit of the hurt is not known to me. Is without end. Is not finite, but is infinite.

"Yet it is conceit, I know. Or at least I think I know it is conceit that causes pain. That I should expect something of you is conceit. That I should expect anything of you is conceit. That I should make demands, and expect you to acquiesce, is. Yet what am I without it? The conceit. Would I love myself? Should I not love myself? Is not my love of myself a part of my love for all other things? For you? That I should want to feel good, not merely good but better than good, not merely better than good, but better than that, and better even than that. To want to feel the most that my nerves can stand, and MORE than they can stand, is that not the measure of my own challenge to the brightest glow of the sun, or the loudest of thunder's grumbles, or . . . or say, can I not want to be all that life is and yet be sane?

"Indeed, this sanity of yours, what has it given us save death, and cries of black or for that matter white?

"But it was you I was talking about . . . or was it?"

It was this note more than anything else they found in John Jr.'s dresser drawer that convinced the judge that John should be sent to Manteno.[7]

KISS OR FORGET
DECEMBER 8, 1959

He'd said all that there was to say. So had she. It was time to kiss her or forget it. Yet not enough, it seemed to him, had been said; not enough assurance had she given him. There was nothing in her manner toward him that said "yes." Definitely "yes." Still there was a vague indefinite yes there in her eyes that dared him. He stared at her, hoping to draw from her face an expression that would give him more of a clue to what he really wanted. She focused her eyes on his and held them there, yet changed her expression no more to accommodate him than she already had.

"Well, I guess I'll be going."

"Okay."

"Uh . . ."

"Huh?"

He stood, stared again; saw, and yet didn't see what she wanted him to do. Said,

---

7. Manteno State Hospital was a psychiatric hospital in Kankakee, Illinois.

"Uh . . ."

"Huh?"

"Uh, goodnite."

It was cold, and dark when he stepped outside, and nobody heard him say to himself,

"You fool. You dog-goned fool!"

OH!
DECEMBER 9, 1959

"Son, do you believe in God?"

"Ye—yessir."

"Do you believe that you will go to hell when you die, if you don't tell the truth?"

"I didn't kill him, suh. Hones' I . . ."

"Look son, we've got five witnesses that swear they saw you do it. Now I'm your friend. Look, have I hurt you?"

"No sir."

"Did I push you around like the other detectives did? Did I?"

"No suh you didn't."

"Now look son, I'm not going to fool you. You are in trouble, serious trouble. Now all we want you to do is admit that you did it. Now like I told you. We know you did it. We got evidence on top of evidence, but I'm just trying to give you a chance to make a clean break. Look, do me a favor will yuh?"

"Yessir."

"Think about God. I mean it. I want you to ask yourself if he would want you to lie about a thing like a murder, 'cause you see, I believe in Him, and I know you do, and I know that if you . . ."

"Lieutenant, sorry to interrupt you."

"What do you want, officer"

"Uh, they got the guy that did it. He confessed the whole thing to the arresting officers."

"Oh."

THE NIGHTMARE[8]
DECEMBER 10, 1959

It had him! He'd run for 30 years, run and hid and changed his face and body and thoughts, and yes, but it had found him and now it had him! It swarmed at him and he moved into a corner. It blew hot air at him and made his stomach empty and caused him to become hungry, and he changed again. This time he turned red and backed into the red corner and thought that his redness and the redness of the corner would hide him, but it did not hide him, and the thing made the roof over his head blow away and in its place was a thin piece of paper with holes in it that let the cold winter in and the writing on the paper said FIVE DAY NOTICE. It actually SAID Five Day Notice. He changed to blue and started singing all the new songs, "That Kind Woman Is the Right Kind of Woman for Me," and "Don't Let the Sun Catch You Crying," but it found him and caused his heels to run down and holes to grow in his soles, so he taught himself to cha-cha-cha, and he turned his hair straight, very, very straight, and he turned his skin white and he cha-cha-cha-ed but it found him and pushed him into the corner, and caused his bare feet to freeze and caused his empty stomach to hurt, and screamed at him over and over again in the bloodless voice of the winter's wind:

"SERVICE WILL BE DISCONTINUED IF PAYMENT IS NOT MADE WITHIN FIVE DAYS!"

QUITTING TIME
DECEMBER 12, 1959

Quitting time was 4:30, and it was quarter to. The men downstairs were rolling! Mattresses slid down the chute as fast as Robbie and the other men on the dock could take them off. Ray Charles was on Robbie's radio singing, "I'm a Fool for You."

Hustling the wrapped mattresses off of the chute, loading them on trucks, and pushing the trucks into the damp, black open mouth of the delivery van, Robbie felt like a young man, not at all like 51.

---

8. Unsigned.

The plant was rolling!

The truck driver tried to lift a mattress off the truck but the others fell against the mattress and the driver, staggering under the weight, called for help. Robbie rushed to help the struggling man.

A little pain, then a big one hit him in the chest. He fell. It was ten minutes to four. The truck had to be loaded before 4:30.

Robbie stared at the faces that bent over him. He tried to rise but couldn't. He tried to talk, but found it hard to move his lips. Straining, he uttered:

"Sh . . . Sherman, get . . . them shippin' orders out my p . . . pocket."

Something by B. B. King came on the radio, and Robbie died just as someone patted his chest for the shipping orders.

THE PLATTER
DECEMBER 14, 1959

". . . and every mother's child will try to spy to see if reindeers really know how to fly."

The song knocked him out. He wiped the glass another wipe, and took another look in the back-bar mirror to see if the light was hitting his hair the right way. It was. The bar was empty. The rent bill, license bill, the tax bill, all lay pierced by the extra-long nail on the wall near the cash register.

Tolly the Jive is the name the customers had given him many double-shots ago. The men stuck the "Tolly" part on, and the women added "The Jive . . ." No one in Tolly the Jive's bar would ever say out loud the last part to The Jive. Like "Jive Stud" or "Jive . . . something else."

Tolly put another dime in the jukebox. The violins seemed to clean up the place. Nat Cole started again, "Shas-nots ro-sting on an open fire . . ."

The longer the record played, the happier Tolly the Jive got. Not a living soul in his place, but the happiness started rising in him, and rising and rising until his head felt light, and for some reason, he wanted to laugh. He breathed deeply, took another look in the mirror; everything seemed so right; so peaceful, so clean.

It was great not to have anybody in the bar.

THE BIG STEP
DECEMBER 15, 1959

The last tears had been cried, the last hand shaken. The last word of warning, and of loving, and of advice had been given. The last bowl of cereal had been cooked, and the last explanation for staying out so late had been given. A handle hung heavy in Cookie's hand. (He'd insisted that they stop calling him "Cookie," and from now on, whenever they addressed him, to call him Clarence!) In the suitcase to which the handle was attached were two new suits, two shirts. Two ties and some underwear. And his toothbrush.

Clarence had pulled the door to, and had walked down the three flights to the vestibule. In his pocket was the uncashed check from his first job. And around his neck underneath his undershirt hung a skate-key. (He'd stopped skating long ago.)

The wind was warm, and there was no drama in the streets over which the dirty papers and crackling leaves blew. Once a tear started in Clarence's neck and hurt it and caused his jaws to feel funny, but he'd swallowed it.

Lifting his foot casually, Clarence too the first step to the sidewalk, and then the second; he turned left, then changed his mind and turned right and took another step, and another, and another and another and another and another.

REALITY
DECEMBER 16, 1959

Reality is. But what IS? And what ISN'T? And who knows how to know what IS and what ISN'T? That is, how does one tell? By touching? By hearing? By smelling? By seeing? Perhaps. Perhaps not. Mamie's problem was more complicated than that. She wanted to know how it is that one knows when one is not loved anymore. Sitting on the couch, she watched Chuck, relaxed in the leather chair near the lamp. She watched the curl of his hair, and the line across his forehead. She followed the quick sweep of his eyes as he peered, fairly bored, into the news of the day. There was nothing new or different about the way he crossed his legs, and when he looked up, catching her looking at him, he smiled, and winked at her, yet it was a motion, and his smile was a smile not an expression of that invisible SOMETHING that she'd known and felt for the many years of their marriage and which now she knew was gone. It all seemed so peaceful, so domestic, so stable and secure, yet there was nothing left, and the room was empty though he was there, and when she started crying, and he got up and rushed to her, she cried even harder.

THE SMELL
DECEMBER 17, 1959

It was the smell of the lake's air that did it. The smell that brought back the memory of Lea and the way she died. Meeting that smell again had not been intentional; rather it had come about as the result of the fog over the lake and the slow, west-going wind that blew into the open side window as he drove along Outer Drive to the Loop.

He turned the radio up louder and a slow song with violins came through. "Thelonious Monk with Strings," he thought. The off chords, and the funny sounding African beat behind the chords, and the strangely contrasting steady, even cry of the strings reminded him of how he'd felt when he'd first taken Lea for a long drive along the lakeside. He laughed, saying aloud, "Bird was playing with strings that day. Strings, strings, who's got the strings."

But it was the smell of the wet, matter-filled lake air, and the hint of fish living and dead for thousands of years, blending now with the smell; it was this more than anything else that caused him to decide to turn off at 47th Street and drive to the 48th Street Station and confess to the hitherto unsolved murder of Lea, age 25.

STOLEN THRILL
DECEMBER 21, 1959

The professor looked behind him. No one was watching. He took his key out, unlocked the door to his room and closed it quickly. He felt the package he'd been carrying under his coat. It was not broken. Pulling the shade down, he walked quickly to his closet and took a stack of records from underneath a carefully laid pile of clothing.

Walking to the door, and pressing his ear against it, he walked back to the records he'd placed on a table. Noises in the early evening were what he'd been waiting for. Upstairs Beethoven's Ninth Symphony rose in broadly chorded majesty, and next door WFMT was fairly soaring with the iconoclastics of Hindemith.[9]

The short white haired man with the strangely flat nose took another look from his window. Seeing no one coming who might interrupt his pleasure, he opened the lop of his portable phonograph, switched it on, laid his latest record on the turntable, went to the couch, took his shoes off, breathed deeply and closed his eyes as the singer started singing.

"A gypsy woman told my mother just before I was born. 'You got a boy child coming . . . gonna be a son of a gun.'"

THE RAVEN
DECEMBER 22, 1959

Black ashes drifted down. Smoke curled, grey and gritty among the smoking, jagged stubs of leafless trees. The sound of falling walls shaken and rent by the bomb's blast thudded over the nightlike afternoon. No man, nor woman, nor child moved save Raymond the Raven.

Sitting on the still hot stone of the steps of the home he'd crawled, staggered, stumbled out of, he swayed from side to side, staring at the crumbled brick and powder of glass broken into fine and myriad particles.

He looked down and saw for the first time that he still held his alto in his hand. Not his wife, nor his son neither, his mother, nor any of his friends, but his alto.

He put it to his mouth, still swaying, sucked it, and spat out the grime, and blew. The first was a long crying whooping howl. The next were ten, maybe fifty fast—lightning fast notes. He stood, leaned on the roofless doorway of his charcoaled house and blew, and blew, and blew. Lifting his horn into the cluttered day gone night, and blew and blew and blew.

---

9. The classical music station, founded in 1948, was playing German composer Paul Hindemith..

THE TRIPLE CROSS
DECEMBER 23, 1960

"Now honey, you know I've never been a jealous woman, but I SAW her in your car."

"I told you; that wasn't me you saw. It must have been somebody who looked like me. I didn't have any woman in my car. So it couldn't have been me."

"Are you trying to say that after three years, I don't know you or your car which, by the way, I helped pay for, when I see it?"

"I'm just saying you didn't see me 'cause I haven't been anywhere with no woman."

"Not even to Cecil and Kermit's?"

"Who told you I was there?"

"Nobody, I saw you."

"Were you following me?"

"No, I just..."

"... happened to be passing."

"Are you trying to be funny honey? I mean finishing my sentences like that?"

"I'm just saying that I'm getting sick and tired of you trying to coop me up like I was a prisoner or something, Maybelle. And as far as you paying for the car..."

"... as far as me paying for the car, forget it. And in fact forget me. In fact you can get out now and go home to your wife or your girlfriend or anybody you please for all I care."

He got up and went back home to his wife.

Even SHE wasn't THAT jealous.

THE DECISION[10]
DECEMBER 24, 1959

The group was set to go. The Chinese were on Hill T. Their mortar fire indicated that someone had zeroed the platoon in. The mortar shots were too accurate. The dead were piling up in the orderly room.

---

10. Unsigned.

Fear was beginning to eat through the unit. The mortar fire had to be stopped. The Chinese had to be attacked.

Dust lingered just above ground as though waiting for the next shot to send it among the splintered limbs of the trees overhead. The sun glaring so hard it reflected off the silicon in the dust and created wobbly rainbows among the tents and gun emplacements facing the Korean North, was but one reason the short, dark, balding lieutenant was busy wiping the sweat from underneath his helmet liner.

The other reason the lieutenant was sweating was that he was to lead the squad into the fire of the Chinese group, and the main reason he was sweating was that in DRAFTING volunteers, he'd started with a group of men in which happened to be his nephew from Mississippi. The image of his mother's face as she explained to him how "Neph" was all her sister had in this world, and that he should take care of "Neph," caused an actual pain in Lt. Higgins' back when he took one look at the long, green, clumsy recruit from home. Yet the problem was this: Should he let "Neph" stay back and make the other men go? Or should he be fair and let "Neph" take his chances?

The lieutenant snapped the snap of the strap under his chin, picked up his rifle, and shouted,

"Fall in, men."

As the men moved to his "forward march!" he, without looking at anyone, said,

"You! 'Home Boy,' go back to the barracks!"

The other men kept marching.

NO JOKE
DECEMBER 28, 1959

It had all started as a joke. He was a friend of the family. Everybody in the building knew him. He was especially a friend of Herman, and when he pecked Diane on the cheek or called her honey, everybody knew that he was just doing it to tease Herman. Herman never got angry. And that is why everyone was so surprised the day they found out that Diane was gone and he was gone and so were their clothes, scrapbooks, checkbooks and bank books.

THE RIDE BACK
DECEMBER 30, 1959

The ride back from the hospital was short and pleasant. Only the harrowing experience of having come back from the door of death caused the stir of fear in Miss Sunday as she stared out of the cab window at South Parkway[11] with its trees, cabs, waste baskets and bus stops going by.

A bout with cancer, she thought, and I beat it, thank God, I beat it! The feeling of triumph, and safety, of luck and power mixed within her and caused her to smile. The driver, catching her eye, smiled at her smile and said,

"I know you glad to be out of that place. I lost a brother there last week, he had cancer."

She tried to look serious, hurt, concerned, but only immense joy that SHE had not died of cancer, that HE had instead of SHE—only the feeling of having been the one chosen to live instead of to die filled her heart, and without being able to control herself, she broke out laughing.

Afterward, the ride the rest of the way was strangely silent.

A CERTAIN SMILE
DECEMBER 31, 1960

Every night at around the same time, 7:30, Coleman, coming home from a hard day in the kitchen at the Loop 24 Hour Restaurant, would glance up at the second floor window to see if his Baby-Sweets was looking. He didn't know her, had never spoken to her, but he'd come to expect her to be sitting at the window for she'd sat there for the solid year he'd been working at the restaurant. Winter, spring, summer and autumn, there she'd be sitting and looking. Once he'd caught her eye, and she'd smiled at him; it was from this time on that he'd started calling her Baby-Sweets like the man on the radio always said.

Each week and month that passed aroused his curiosity, and with the heightening of his curiosity and the way she smiled at him—once she even waved—he decided one day to go up and see her. Perhaps

---

11. South Parkway was the original name of Martin Luther King Jr. Drive.

he'd even tell her that he called her Baby-Sweets, perhaps even that he loved her and would like to see her, and, well, a lot of things.

Climbing the stairs, knocking on the door, and asking the old lady with the slight mustache about the woman "upstairs," he found himself unable to think or speak when the woman gently told him,

"Oh, you must be mistaken, that was my daughter's room but she's been dead for a year."

JUST "TOO MUCH"
JANUARY 4, 1960

Although Mrs. Cross had enough junk in her living room to fill a second-hand store, even she was getting tired of that big, ugly bronze bust of a fat woman in a big hat. The bronze had turned a sickly green, and even the bronze lady seemed to be sick at the stomach. In other words, Mrs. Cross decided one bright and early morning that the green-bronze lady in the big hat had to go!

Much to her surprise, the secondhand dealer gave her three dollars for it.

Sitting happily, quietly rejoicing over the fact that it was her birthday, though equally as much because she was rid of that green woman, Mrs. Cross was even happier when her son and daughter-in-law rushed in, kissed her, laid her birthday present on the table and waited for her to open it.

Eagerly unwrapping it, Mrs. Cross swallowed, smiled and fainted when she stared at the brightly polished bust of her old friend—the green lady with the big hat.

Her daughter-in-law said,

"We thought you might like the twin to your lady with the hat."

But Mrs. Cross didn't hear a word she said.

DIG, YOU GOOFED
JANUARY 5, 1960

"Dig, Jim, you goofed! I mean like you was supposed to meet me at two-thirty this morning and you show up at two-thirty this evening. I mean like what's happening? Have you broke your habit? I mean like don't you need anything anymore?"

"Dig, Baby, I'm sorry. I just couldn't make it. I tried to wake up this morning but ... dig baby, I couldn't make it. You know?"

"The watchman leaves at two-thirty every night. I think he got a broad. Anyway you BE there tonight."

"Or else?"

"Or else you get wasted baby."

"I'll be there."

The next night the policemen with whom the watchman had been playing cards decided to play in the supermarket so the watchman wouldn't have to keep going back and forth whenever he ran out of money. This is how they happened to hear Baby sneaking in. And this is how they happened to fill him with lead.

As usual Jim[12] goofed. He overslept again and did not show.

AMONG THIEVES
JANUARY 6, 1960

"You won't regret it doctor, I know. You're not just testifying against a friend, you're testifying against a danger to the community. Thanks again. We'll see you in court."

This conversation hummed and replayed itself in the doctor's mind all the while he tried to close the ruptured kidney of the dark, fat, conked-hair man on the operating table before him.

The lights from an incoming ambulance silhouetted the bars at the window of the prison hospital upon his face and upon the inert body before him.

Detectives stood in the shadows whispering.

"Did you have to hit him so hard?"

"How was I to know? All he had to do was tell us where the 'connect' is. You know he knows. Why wouldn't he tell?"

"These addicts ... well, some of them would die first."

The doctor felt the addict's last flutter of life. He laid his instruments

---

12. The names in these two paragraphs were originally switched, but judging by the last two paragraphs, where Baby shows up but Jim goofs "as usual," that was in error.

beside the body and left the room.

Going to court tomorrow would be even harder now.

IMMORTALITY
JANUARY 7, 1960

At the very day, hour and second Belle died, Clarice was born on Forty-Seventh Street. At the very day, hour and second Clarice died, David was born on Forty-Eighth Street. At the very day, hour and second David died, Edward was born on Forty-Ninth Street. At the very day, hour and second Edward died, Fred was born on Fiftieth Street. At the very day, hour and second Fred died, Gladys was born on Fifty-First Street. At the very day, hour and second Gladys died, Herman was born on Fifty-Second Street. At the very day, second and hour Herman died, Irving was born on Fifty-Third Street. And then came J, K, L, M, N, O, P, Q, R, S, T, U, V, W, X, Y, and Z, and beyond there, beyond the numbers, beyond the letters, beyond all time and all things, and all distance . . . when one stepped out, one stepped in.

World without beginning. World without end.

WELL?
JANUARY 12, 1960

Sinatra was through and Joe Williams was starting up with "Gee Baby, Ain't I Good to You."

The sun was laying atop all things that Tab could see from the wide window. And the discoloration that turned grey to magenta, and black to rose-rust, created a mood that seemed to yell, "Well?"

"Well?" was in her eyes too. And over all the room; over her, and the deep hip crying of Joe Williams singing softly from the hi-fi.

WELL? The sun said. WELL. The room and the world around him said. WELL? said her still and hand-carved face.

He smiled, sat up, lit a cigarette; blew the smoke toward the wall across the room, groped for words, and finding none that would say the thing right, wondered, simply wondered how one tells a woman that her YES was sufficient. And that the room, the music, and the sun . . . she in fact had given him already all he'd ever really dreamed of wanting. He wanted nothing else, and could not pretend that he wanted anything else.

FORCE OF HABIT
JANUARY 13, 1960

So it had happened to him! He'd seen her with Quinton[13]; had seen them holding hands; had seen her kiss him. No rumor told him this. No imagination created this. A quiet, secluded corner in an out of the way place, and his decision to follow his wife, Sandra, had brought this realization to him face to face and point blank.

Stepping before them, Marlon smiled, looking steadily at Sandra and then Quinton.

"Fancy meeting you here—together."

Sandra's face had the proper look of shock, fear and remorse, yet she was calm when she spoke,

"I'm sorry you had to find out like this, Marlon."

"After ten years, all you can say is that you're sorry. What happened to our ten years? Skunk, I'm through. Don't explain. Forget it!"

He turned quickly and walked away.

Outside the wind blew down his neck and he remembered how Sandra used to rub his back whenever they walked down the street. He remembered many things.

He stopped, turned around; went back into the restaurant and to Sandra. He was crying, but did not know it. He said, softly,

"Sandra, can I speak to you a minute, please?"

THE TIME
JANUARY 14, 1960

When the time came for the boy to marry the girl, he started thinking. Days at the Avenue, nights at McKie's and the Pershing,[14] cha-

---

13. This originally said Marlon, but it appears that was an error.

14. McKie's Disk Jockey Lounge was located at Sixty-Third and Cottage Grove in the Strand Hotel. The Pershing Hotel, at Sixty-Fourth and Cottage Grove, housed a ballroom (now the Grand Ballroom), a lounge, and a nightclub.

cha-cha-ing up on Sixty-Third—all this came back to him as a warning finger, wagging its warning in the solemn gesture of mother telling junior, "Don't do it!"

Big Benny thought about all this while driving to Della's house; while going there to tell her the something "important" he'd promised to tell her.

When he reached Della's house he'd made up his mind. Not right now. Let's wait and make sure. We shouldn't rush into a thing like this. Big B. pushed the doorbell, waited and was beginning to smile at Della as she led him into the living room when he saw the one he KNEW Della once went for. Suddenly the Pershing, McKie's and the Avenue seemed unimportant. Suddenly only marrying Della before Mr. Handsome got her mattered. Suddenly he found himself blurting:

"Well, I came over here to ask you to marry me. Are you or aren't you?"

Della lit up, hugged him and squealed:

"Oh yes, honey. This is really something! Handsome, here, got married last month himself. Isn't that funny?"

LIKE FATE, MAYBE
JANUARY 18, 1960

They were young and they were walking down Madison Avenue, "skid row."

"You know, these people really get next to you, don't they?"

"Yeah they do, but it's their own fault. If they really wanted to live better, they could find jobs and make a life for themselves. This 'bum' stuff is for the birds. I say like, suffer, no better for yuh."

The first man that asked them for money was an old man with long grey hair, and a look in his eye of past strength, hope and faith gone dry. They walked past him, without looking at him. They were arguing about the "real problems."

"So, you think it's their own fault: Well, I don't agree. I think it's something bigger than all of us, something bigger than anything; like fate maybe."

They passed another man who had held his hands out to them, and had walked beside them for a few steps and had mumbled,

"Please."

"Well, fate or not, I feel that as young people the future is in our hands, and we should try to make the world a better place in which to live."

And both young men nodded in agreement as they passed another beggar without noticing him.

SHE SMILED
JANUARY 20, 1960

Terrence was sick, but he tried not to think too much about it. He sat down at the table and waited for Marge to bring him another one of the delicious meals she'd been cooking lately. It was Sunday and he waited eagerly for whatever goodies she was about to bring.

A pain, the same pain he'd been feeling for about two weeks, split, it seemed, his stomach into little ribbons. He gripped his stomach with both hands; the pain went away. Marge came in with his meal. She was smiling. That smile hurt him, especially after he'd busted her in the mouth not long ago.

The meal started coming in in a steady build up of smells, colors, and temperatures. Crusty, brown ham, speckled with spicy sweet cloves; sweet potatoes, macaroni, golden with melted cheese; asparagus, okra, cucumbers, beets, hot rolls fuming in the mist of melted butter.

Terrence didn't wait for her to finish the flow of food. He started into the meal, stuffing the ham, potatoes, beets into his mouth. His stomach groaned and ached, but the food was too delicious to think about that now. Pies and cakes came in, and wines. Terrence ate and ate and ate, keeping his eye upon the vanishing piles of food on his plate. The pain in his stomach grew worse and Terrence finally had to stop eating. He looked up at Marge to say that he felt terrible.

It was then that the look of total, consuming hatred in her eyes caused him to look from her to the food, and back at her again.

The pain slashed at his stomach again, and he looked at Marge just once more, horrified, and stunned. She smiled.

A WRONG-DOER
JANUARY 21, 1960

There was nothing nobody could tell her about Fifty-Eighth Street. She knew that everybody on the street was a wrong-doer and she was holding on to her purse for dear life as she stepped out of the "L" station and headed toward Calumet. The fact that it was dark didn't help her any; and the fact that she had an arm-load of packages she picked up on her once-a-week shopping tour, didn't make holding on to her purse any easier. Which is why she dropped her purse. She didn't see the chubby, dark-skinned man pick it up. She was just going! Getting away from "these people."

The chubby man called her. She heard him, but she didn't turn, just walked faster.

The chubby man walked fast trying to catch up with her. She walked even faster.

The chubby man ran after her, she screamed, dropped the packages, and broke out!

A man came out of the store just in time to catch sight of the chubby man with the purse in his hands, and the woman running down the street screaming. He tackled the chubby man, knocked him down, and held him there on the sidewalk until the police came. The chubby man got thirty days.

JUST PEOPLE
JANUARY 25, 1960

So everybody was friends at the factory alright, but that still didn't mean that the whites did not know they were white and the Negroes did not know they were Negro. They talked and kidded around and all that, but when it came to getting personal, everybody rather cooled it—as it were.

Widow Louise was beginning to get over the loss of her husband. She'd begun to tell the foremen off again, and once, somebody even caught her whistling. The love had been deep, and three years had gone by before you knew it. And Louise was whistling at the time she'd left her seat at the cafeteria table to get a piece of cake she'd left at her machine.

When she came back, Landis, a middle aged white man, was sitting in her seat.

When he saw her, he smiled, got up, and found another chair for her, beside him.

The women teased her about this after lunch. She snapped back, "You must be crazy. Me? With him? Girl you ARE crazy."

But it happened the next day, the same way, and the next; which is why no one was surprised when, a little later on, one of the girls received a nice white, embossed invitation to a wedding.

ALMOST
JANUARY 27, 1960

There was nothing wrong with him, actually. He was tired. The couch felt good. She was in the kitchen cooking. The house was warm. His mind started to wander. He let himself go limp. Focused his eyes on the ceiling and stared at and past the ceiling, past all things, past his own mind even. Stared and started to plunge; yet it seemed as though he could control it. Still he chose to go into this secret and cold place that his mind had discovered. Down he went, and down, and his body began to hum, and he felt as though the molecules and atoms of him were moving away from each other and into the molecules of the cold and secret world around him. He felt himself blending with the air, and the dust and the unseen things about him. He knew that he had entered into a fearful place, and that he might never return. He tried to pull himself out, but the grip on him was too great. He tried to open his eyes, but somehow realized that they were already open. He tried to scream but found that he could not. He tried to turn and toss, but nothing happened.

"Honey, are you ready to eat dinner?"

A thin bubble popped. He was free! He sat up. Got up. Smiled, stretched.

"Oh yes. I AM hungry. I am so happy . . . I mean hungry."

THE FOREMAN[15]
JANUARY 28, 1960

So there he lay, with oil and blood puddled beside his head; a break in his scalp; a break in his skull . . . dead.

Sitting on the lip of a still sewing machine, Ortho Coleman stared into the open eyes of Turner, the man he'd killed. Everybody in the shop stood around him—around Turner. None talked. Everyone waited for the police. Ortho let fall the wrench with which he'd struck Turner. The "brang" made everybody jump. Somebody laughed. The argument had been so quick—so brief.

"Take this finished ticks down to the fillers."

"That ain't my job, man."

"So what. I'm your foreman. Take that stuff to the fillers."

"You must be crazy or something. You jive cat . . . shee-it, ain't you some stuff, as poor and raggedy as YOU are."

"Who you talkin' to huh? Huh! Huh?"

And between each "huh" he hit Turner. Give him everything he had. So there he lay, with oil and blood puddled beside his head; a break in his scalp; a break in his skull . . . dead.

"Ortho, you didn't have to hit him. You should have called me. After all, I'm the owner of this plant, remember?"

Ortho nodded. He remembered.

ASHLAND, RIGHT
FEBRUARY 1, 1960

The car was warm, and Al Benson was on. The other cars on the Congress Street Expressway[16] were scooting over the yellow lines, and all around. She didn't sit near him. She didn't want to; not now anyway.

"Are you sure you want to go through with it?"

"What choice have we got?"

"Sweetheart, I know we haven't got much choice, but maybe you

---

15. Unsigned.

16. The Congress Street Expressway was the original name of the Eisenhower Expressway, US-290, which opened in 1955.

could just . . . well, just have it."

"No. If we can't be together I don't want it."

"We went through all that, remember?"

"Then I'm going through with it."

"I hear it's dangerous."

"l imagine so."

The green sign overhead read FOR ASHLAND, KEEP RIGHT. She laughed.

"For Ashland, keep right. How does one keep 'right' these days?"

The car moved to the right of the Expressway, and turned into the driveway that led up to Ashland.

"Sweetheart, I . . . I wish I knew what else we could do?"

"We?"

No one spoke for the rest of the way.

NO "FOREVER"[17]
FEBRUARY 2, 1960

What is there to say when your lover is gone and the hole she left is left wringing in the singing and the ringing wind? Or when she has left there at its bottom (the hole's) a tiny quivering thing or nothing that beats and hurts and burns till her absence is like her presence and her presence is like her absence? That is when she has caused the maps and charts, and compasses in you to go wrong, or really, to go.

Is it loneliness? Or is it the bitter taste of a foreign object, that object being her difference, her change, her foreign-ness? Then what is loneliness? What is darkness? What is cold on the inside of you? What is the feeling of being nowhere? Belonging to no one, and knowing no one belongs to you? That someone has not died, but has simply changed in that way died, and no longer is yours—familiar . . . is "foreign?"

Yet what does one keep forever . . . intact? A wife? A child? A lover? A mother? A father? What? Nothing? Perhaps. Nothing stays, little remains for long. There is no "forever." The word itself is man's arms stretched against matter's great girth . . . only against it; never around it; never encompassing it, or himself, or his loves, or his women, or his dreams.

17. Unsigned.

THE "NAZI"
FEBRUARY 10, 1960

"There ain't no dinner! There ain't no dinner! So don't bother me about it! I'm broke. Daddy ain't home and there ain't no dinner. Get out of here! I'm sick and tired. I . . ."

Ronny backed out, ran down the stairs, stopped at the landing, turned, looked up and backed out into the streets.

"Shoot, no dinner last night. No dinner tonight. Shoot."

He stepped on a Coke bottle.

"Two cents. I mo get me the deposit and get some cookies, shoot."

He looked at his shadow on the wall of the building at Fifty-Eighth and Calumet as he turned onto Fifty-Eighth Street. He was fifteen but he looked seventeen.

The Aces were coming from Fifty-Ninth and Calumet. They were after him. He ran. They saw him, they ran, but he outran them and stopped at Fifty-Fifth Street, bottle still in his hand. A newspaper slipped to the pavement from a man's arm.

Ronny picked it up, made a move to call the man, stopped, and said, "Later for the square."

The headline of the paper talked about the swastikas. He'd liked swastikas from the days of the war movies on television. Swastika and black boots, and the sharp tanks in the Egyptian desert.

Re-read about the swastikas while leaning against the tavern at Fifty-Fifth and Indiana. His stomach started growling. He remembered the bottle in his hand. He looked around for a delicatessen, found one and entered it.

The white man with the glasses and the white hair-band around his big bald head, said,

"No deposits today."

He left.

"Shoot."

He picked up a white brick and marked a swastika on the side of the wall.

"Shoot."

THE NEW BABY[18]
FEBRUARY 11, 1960

The baby was pretty alright, but it meant more nights of formulas, diapers, and crying. It was that crying that did it. It wasn't as if Maybelle didn't love the baby. It was not that at all. Maybelle looked at the clock. Two o'clock in the morning. She put the iron to the diaper, lit a cigarette, and thought about the good old days at DuSable. Sweet Charlie Brown, Curley Johnson, the screaming and the cheering downstate when the team won the really important games and finally the state title. "Go team go!"

Sid McCoy's program went off the air.[19] The house was warm. The cigarette was burning slowly. Martin, her husband, was asleep in the bedroom. She went to sleep, cigarette still burning, dreaming about the good old days. The fire from the butt caught the nap of the rug, and the flame in smoke and orange light. The baby started crying, but Maybelle slept on. The fire licked upwards from the rug, and the baby cried even louder. Maybelle tried to put the crying out of her mind. But the crying would not go out of her mind. The habit of motherhood was too strong and she opened one eye, and after a while, the other eye. She caught the smell of smoke, and the brightness of the fire shocked her to action. Grabbing a pail, she rushed to the sink, filled it, and doused the fire. The baby was still crying. It was the cry which saved her life.

THE ARGUMENT
FEBRUARY 15, 1960

It exploded so suddenly, seemingly without cause. The receptionist had asked a question. Herman had answered it. He'd asked a question; some other words had passed and in seconds the argument had begun.

She was lean, ascetic, full featured, brisk, hard. He was husky frown-

18. Unsigned.

19. The multi-talented McCoy was a jazz DJ, the announcer on *Soul Train*, a producer at Chicago's Vee-Jay Records, and an actor.

ing, bullish, angry.

"Miss, I answered that question once. If you'd been listening, you would have heard me the first time."

"Well, sir, just answer the questions. We're not here to run a debating contest."

"And I didn't come to enter a debating contest. I simply want to see the doctor."

"I didn't say you were here to enter a debating contest. I said..."

"I know what you said. And if you weren't trying so hard to be smart, you'd..."

"All that yelling isn't necessary."

"It certainly was necessary. And another thing..."

The receptionist started laughing. He started laughing. They laughed together. He looked at her. She looked at him. This time they smiled. Then they looked at each other, and didn't smile at all. They simply looked, each into the eyes of the other. And when he placed his hand on the counter, it touched her hand. She didn't move her hand. He didn't move his hand.

JAMIE
FEBRUARY 17, 1960

They'd found out. No longer the slightest doubt. The survivors were threatened again. Salvation from the devastation of the H-bomb blast was still not the end of their troubles. The doctors who'd led the party to the island when they'd detected the X-Magnitude light blast at Hawaii, now found that typhoid was the new danger. Two of the twenty had died; all were tested—one was found to be a carrier of the disease. That one had to be removed. They stood in the doorway of the hut where the one lived; they talked to a tall, tired woman whose eyes were black with the exhaustion and worry of attending her sick ten year old son, Jamie.

"Mrs. Murdock, we've no doubt in our minds. Right now, no one else in the group has it. Those who did have it have died. We've checked and rechecked our findings. We know that if the person who is carrying the disease remains among us, perhaps we will all contract it and die. We may be the only humans left in the world alive. We don't know, but we cannot let this small group die as long as there is anything which can be done about the danger to the group."

Mrs. Murdock felt fear, and trembled, but she still managed to ask, "Why did you come here?"

"Mrs. Murdock, the typhus carrier must be eliminated from our midst."

"I . . . understand. I . . . I'll go."

"He must be killed, Mrs. Murdock. We cannot take a chance."

"HE must be killed! Jamie? HE? My son? Killed? HE? HE?"

"We are very sorry, Mrs. Murdock. The fate of mankind depends up . . ."

But Mrs. Murdock didn't hear the rest.

MONDAY MORNING
FEBRUARY 18, 1960

At no time had life seemed drearier; at no time did a decision seem harder to make. There was no one to help her. No voice advised her. No face whose expression told her what was best. It was a lonely decision. The covers of her bed grew heavy upon her. The room's darkness grew blacker. The sounds seemed to recede and advance and repeat the slushing movements as of waves upon a nearby shore: cars, footsteps of people passing by, voices a room or a block away: all coming and going but staying away from the enclosure of her solitude so that nothing influenced her decision.

She turned toward the wall, and back again toward the luminous clock on the stand near her bed. The wind seemed angry and shoved the window. This didn't make the decision any easier to be arrived at. Finally she opened one eye, then the other. Next she slid one foot to the edge of the bed, then out of the bed, and then the other foot. Painfully she lifted the covers away and the room's cold stuck to her and caused her to shiver. She stood. She looked around the dark room and at the clock. It read: six o'clock! She yawned, stretched, and turned on the light. She was up! She had made the decision. She had actually gotten up!

THE LETTER
FEBRUARY 23, 1960

The wagon was driving faster than usual. Roger had always had trouble sitting on that narrow ledge, and now that it was fairly sailing down South Parkway, he really had trouble.

He took a letter out from among the papers he'd stumbled upon while fumbling through his pockets, trying to do something to kill his nervousness. Going to jail made him nervous. It always had.

"Dear Roger,

"I'm glad to know that you've done a lot of thinking about things since you have been there. I agree, there is no shortcut to a good life. You are right when you say that honesty is the best policy. And what you said about living up to God . . . trying to be a Christian is the most wonderful thing you ever said. I hope you really meant it this time. I believe you do. The kids are fine, and they miss their Daddy. I do, too. So hurry home, so we can have that pot of gold at the end of the rainbow which you mentioned in your last letter. I thought that was real cute. Well, must go now. Answer soon."

The wagon stopped; the door opened. He got out, looked around him, breathed deeply once as the policemen took him to the Sergeant's desk. He glanced only once at the crumpled letter he'd dropped at the door of the station.

THE PROPOSAL
FEBRUARY 24, 1960

"No one really expects to miss a brother."

Red didn't say this, but the thought was there just the same. He stared across the room at the big graduation diploma from DuSable; framed and hung on the wall right above the television, it itself looked like the screen of a television set. In it Red could see Mannie, his big brother, walking down the aisle at DuSable, and then down the aisle at Tabernacle Baptist church.

Married! It just didn't seem right that there'd be no more double-dating, and hay-rides, and skating parties.

Red looked at the palm of his left hand. Mannie had a ring on HIS left hand now. No one else was at home. The house's quiet made the loneliness worse. Red thought about Patricia. THEY HAD talked about getting married. He thought about Jennette, THEY'D—he and she had—talked about getting married. Who shall it be? Patricia? Jennette? He picked up the phone and started dialing; at first not knowing who he was dialing. A girl answered. It was Jennette.

"Uh, hullo, uh Jennette. Can l come over? I mean, there's something I'd like to talk to you about. It's very important. Okay, I'll be over right after dinner . . . 'bye."

THE END
FEBRUARY 25, 1960

He Was Thinking: I'm tired of this . . . stuff. I cannot take it anymore. I'm leaving. I am leaving her. I must.

She Was Thinking: Maybe I shouldn't be so hard on him. After all, he's going to do what he's going to do. There's no need to nag him. But God! It's hard to take. But I'm going to take it. I've got to. I do still love him.

He Was Thinking: Well, let's see; how will I tell her?

She Was Thinking: Well, let's see. What will I fix him that's really good to eat?

He Was Thinking: When she gets up, I'll call her, and I'll say, "Honey, we just can't make it anymore. I'm sorry. I know it's a drag, but I'm leaving. You can have everything; house, car, Hi-Fi, everything. I'm sorry, but that's how it is."

She Was Thinking: I know. I'll fix him his favorite: red beans, rice, and corn bread with lots of hot butter.

She got up. He coughed. She smiled at him. He smiled at her. She started to walk toward the kitchen. He said,

"Honey, we just can't . . ."

And the words went on and on and on.

THE WARRIOR
FEBRUARY 29, 1960

It wouldn't have been so bad if the place had not charged a two fifty cover charge. Not to speak of the fact that he was making his speech at the same time Ornette was breaking out into one of those musical rashes that split notes all over the place. But this stud was upset about Mack Parker,[20] and so we had to listen, 'cause the fact that we'd been upset too. But it had been at least 10 months ago that Parker had been lynched and so we'd gotten our minds on other things and right now it was Ornette Coleman.

"Yes, if we'd only stick together. I mean we could do wonders. That's why the white man thinks he can do anything he wants to, to us right today, 'cause we don't stick together. Shucks..."

Meanwhile Ornette is wailing and none of us can hear him!

"Shucks, why I remember when I was down home. I ain't shamed to say I'm from Miss. Sippi. A white man didn't think about callin' me out of my name. That's why I'm up here right today. A ol' boy was in some trouble with one of them white women. She liked him if you want to know the truth, and these peckerwoods was gon' lynch that boy and I was staying with him and his ol' momma at the time and they come to that do' and I got my shotgun and I stood in the do' and I said 'If you want him, you got to take me first.' Shucks you shoulda seen..."

He stopped talking suddenly. We looked in the direction in which he stared for an explanation of his sudden silence. We found it.

A tall, husky white policeman in uniform was approaching. He passed. The young warrior continued,

"Yes, don't tell me nothing about..."

We all got up at the same time and walked away.

---

20. Mack Charles Parker was a Black man who was lynched in Pearl River County, Mississippi, on April 24, 1959.

ORNETTE'S WEIRD
MARCH 2, 1960

Ornette Coleman was standing on the stand blowing a yellow plastic saxophone. The air coming out of the sax's open end blew the smoke that hung around the ceiling and around Ornette's horn. It gave Jackie the impression of water gushing through thick gray clouds, disturbing them only a little as it pushed up and outward to nowhere.

Jackie listened to the wine-like dizziness that curled from the horn in the form of sound. Notes took him along the path of the melody, and without any warning left him on the path while it veered off and away into some crying, off-toned side-trail where only Charlie Parker and Thelonious Monk had ventured.

Jackie's eyes kept sliding down across his face and he had to clench his fists and strain to make them crawl back up into his eye sockets. His head kept tip-toeing down to his chest where, it seemed, his head wanted to have words with something in his chest. But Jackie pulled a string at the back of his neck and his head walked back onto his shoulders.

Ornette started walking off the stand . . . off the edge. Just walking, in air . . . on nothing. Just walking and blowing things at him. Jackie knew that Ornette wouldn't fall. He knew that Ornette could fly if he wanted to, but he didn't think that it was nice for Ornette to be walking on air while everybody was looking. And so he got up and flew to where Ornette was, so that he could tell him not to walk on air while everybody was looking.

It was then that someone called him a "junkie" and threw him out onto Drexel Blvd.

OLD WOMAN
MARCH 3, 1960

Weeds grew up around the kitchenette as though it were a mansion on a dead southern plantation. A wind sang in the same key over the far sound of children laughing and dishes clinking and cars passing.

The building's walls were old, like old skin on an old and abused woman. Wrinkles caved in the surface of the building's skin, and blackened, by the passing wind-blown dirt, criss-crossed like the lines an old woman's face does when she smiles or cries.

A crow landed on a sill on the third floor and above the crow a raised window with the glass still in it, gleamed like the only tooth in a hag's mouth.

The basement door gaped open, its door, wide, loose, sagging, as though many children had gone through it.

No one came to see her anymore. No one wanted to go inside her and take her warmth, or look through her eyes, or smell her or touch her. She was not down, broken up, and buried beneath the fresh green of a new parking lot, or a young, fertile building with rooms to hold many babies—yet she was not dead.

And so she stood among the weeds of her isolation, and not even a rat would go inside her.

EMMETT'S GHOST
MARCH 7, 1960

Tall and alone she stood at Michigan and Chicago Avenue. All the people said, "I'll be home for Christmas." A Fourth of July rocket burst the red glare of the sun with a blue gleam of its own. The noise and the blue caught the tall girl's eye and she smiled at the young man who'd walked by whistling. "I'll be home for Christmas."

It had seemed as though all the people had said it, when actually only one had, and even he had not said it, nor sang it, but had whispered it, or rather whistled it, but had only seemed to be whispering it to her.

"Taxi, ma'm?"

"Take me to the colored section!"

"The colored section?"

What he didn't say was, "But you're white."

What he did say was, "Yes, ma'm!"

Sixty-Third and Cottage Grove was what the cab driver thought of as the most colored of sections he'd ever taken anybody to, so it was where he took her.

She got out of the cab, paid him and walked into the street just as a car going through the green light neared her. She stepped into the car's path; the car swerved away from her, but she leaped again into its path, and for a second or so, she and the car did a kind of elephant's waltz. The car hit her. She died. No one claimed the body.

THE DAY DREAM
MARCH 8, 1960
SHORT, SHORT FEATURE[21]

Witches' nights lay with him as he slipped down long and black holes with wet walls, and ticks that sounded of mice in clocks ramming their whiskers against the second hand spring and the springs of the hourly and minute hand.

Each breath was blood and the taste in his mouth was talking with separate and nipping mouths. He was drowning in his breath and listening to the noise in his mouth when a woman opened the door of his head and peeped in; seeing no one there, she called him to dinner.

He smiled up at her though she was some distance away and he could really make out only the outline of her head as she moved away from his sight and closed the top of his head.

A voice ate his ear and started on the other one. The words were teeth and they chewed and munched until he finally turned the light in his eyes back on, and focused them on the eye of the face which mumbled at his ear,

"Senator; senator . . . it's your turn to take up the filibuster, sir."

"What filibuster?"

"Why the filibuster against the civil rights bill, sir."

"Oh . . . yes . . . yes, that's right."

The senator stood,

"Gentlemen, I rise to affirm what my honorable colleagues have said. States' rights are the most sacred . . ."

His head began to clear after he'd been talking for about an hour.

---

21. Brown wrote a few stories that appeared as "Short, Short Feature" or "Short, Short Story" instead of under the "This Is Life" banner.

THE RIDDLE
MARCH 9, 1960

"Wherever the wind blows and the water moves before it, and the light of the moon doubles in the ruffles of the mirror of the lake, the sound of life shall follow. But when the wind is still and no water moves, and no light moves upon the wave, you shall hear a step upon the sand and the god of the night will approach you. He will ask you but one question which you must answer. If you do not answer, you shall sink beneath the sands and be like the sand, and of the sand. You shall vanish from this earth and all earths until time is no more and no one shall speak your name."

It was a kind of dream he'd been having, or seemed to remember that he'd had as he stared up at the man standing over him with his back to the moon. The man spoke to him,

"What are you doing out here?"

"I . . . I'm just on the beach, officer."

"I know where you are. A woman was raped out here last week. What are you doing on this earth . . . uh, beach?"

"I . . . I was just lying down."

"What are you doing on this earth . . . uh, beach?"

The officer was screaming. His hand slipped his gun from the holster. He pointed it at the man on the beach.

"If you don't answer my question, I'll blow your brains out!"

The man knew that he wouldn't be able to answer the question . . . he waited for the blast of the gun.

THE MISTAKE
MARCH 15, 1960

When the time came to get up, Sergeant Gibson stood stiffly. The officers of the court martial sat about the table, stern, silent, and full of a secret they all knew.

"What have you to say for yourself, sergeant? Did you or did you not refuse to order your men to charge the hill?"

"I thought there were colored men on that hill, sir. They looked to me to be colored."

"They were Koreans, sergeant, and you had your orders. You caused the death of half of C Battalion."

"The light was bad. Something happened to my eyes. I thought that they were black men, sir. I . . . I really did."

"They were not black men, sergeant. They were Koreans."

"I made a mistake, sir."

"You certainly did, sergeant."

The order for the execution was given quickly, curtly, and with a businesslike air. The time passed quickly. The sergeant was shot. He'd paid for his mistake.

LAST ARGUMENT
MARCH 21, 1960

And when the moon passed into the clouds, the man went to bed. His wife was asleep, but she awoke when he got into bed.

"What's the matter, honey?"

"Oh, nothing. I didn't mean to wake you up."

"You didn't wake me up. I woke up after I realized that you hadn't come to bed yet."

"I didn't mean to disturb you."

"Why didn't you come to bed?"

"I don't know."

"I hope I haven't done anything else wrong."

"No you haven't. Please let's not argue anymore tonight."

"Am I arguing now?"

"No . . . not now."

"Well, . . . good night."

"Good night."

"Mary . . ."

"Huh?"

"I'm sorry."

But Mary was asleep—just that quick, and she didn't awaken until the poison had begun to work, and his kicking, and twisting, broke through her dreams. By then it was too late.

LOVE II[22]
MARCH 22, 1960

"Aw, don't tell me. I know you been out with that . . ."

"Listen, Maybelle, I'm not goin' to lay here and let you accuse me. Every time I step out the house, you think I'm going out with some . . ."

". . . skunk, Richard. That's just what I think, and another thing, you been messin' up with the money. This is the second week you've come home with some jive excuse. Last week you were robbed. This week, the man at the currency exchange short-changed you."

"Well, if you tired of what I'm puttin' down, either I'll leave or you can leave. I don't care which, Maybelle. I ain't gon' spend the rest of my life arguing with you; fifteen years of fighting is long enough."

"Well, ain't that late. Now that I got a house full of babies to take care of, YOU say if we can't get along we can just forget it. Man, I'll blow your brains out before I let you get out of this."

"You'll what?"

"You heard me."

"I just want to hear you say that again."

"The next time I say it, you might be sorry."

"You sure are a jive broad."

"Who are you callin' a broad? Is that what you call your . . ."

"Don't talk about my family."

"I didn't say anything about . . ."

It was about this time that Richard fell asleep. Shortly afterwards Maybelle fell asleep. They turned toward each other in their sleep and Maybelle raised her head and Richard put his arm under it, and soon Richard was snoring the way he had for fifteen years.

LOVE III
MARCH 23, 1960

The bread truck, and milk truck, pop truck, and vegetable truck, rounded Calumet from Fifty-Seventh, and stopped at the huddle of stores on Fifty-Eighth Street.

---

22. "Love I" does not seem to have been printed.

Mr. DeThomas took a little of his weight off his cane and straightened his back a bit as a young woman passed him, heading for the 8:00 a.m. Englewood loop-bound "L."

"Good morning partner."

"Ho, Mr. Wilson! I didn't see you come up behind me."

"You were too busy looking at that young chick."

"Well, now, I've seen you blink your eyes at many a young chick."

The talk went into noon. The children rushed by them, going home for lunch.

"DeThomas, these youngsters these days are smart as whippersnappers. You hear what that mannish little thing said just now?"

"I heard him, Wilson. It's all this TV and jet planes and..."

"... no God in their lives. That's the main thing."

"Awww, come on, Wilson. I know what you think about stuff like that."

Evening brought the young lady back again. Her face lined just a bit more, and her steps a bit slower. Her expression more grim.

"Well, I reckon it's time to get on back. DeThomas, do you know it's almost six o'clock?"

"Darned if it isn't. Well, I'll see you tomorrow."

"See you tomorrow."

LOVE IV
MARCH 24, 1960

"I didn't say that she could make better cakes than you, I said..."

"Well, Arnetta, I'm not saying you did say that. I'm just saying that you never did rave over any of my cakes like that."

"I didn't rave over her cake. I just said it was the best cake OF ITS KIND that I've eaten in a long time."

"I know, but I've cooked every kind of cake in the world. You know that!"

"But not that kind."

"What kind is that?"

"Strawberry ice cake."

"Ha! I've never even heard of a strawberry ice cake!"

"It was very good."

"Well, if you're going to throw our friendship out the window just because a stranger gives you a piece of a funny-style cake…"

"Just a minute, Arnetta; I'm not throwing our friendship out the window. I think you're acting awfully silly in the first…"

"Now I'm silly! After all we've been friends since before you even met Horace. I've seen you through thick and thin, and…"

"So what's that got to do with a piece of cake?"

"Oh, forget it!"

"I think we should, Arnetta."

"Are you going to club meeting tomorrow?"

"Yes."

"Well, I'll pick you up at six o'clock sharp."

"I'm always on time."

"Six o'clock, Arnetta?"

"Six o'clock."

MERCIFUL JUDGE[23]
MARCH 28, 1960
SHORT, SHORT FEATURE

In the darkness of a clothing store, of Middleboro, Mass., with an open cash box before him, 23-year-old William Perry forgot that he was a policeman.

Instead, he admitted later, his mind flashed back to his poorly furnished apartment where his son, four-year-old William, Jr., was slowly dying of cancer.

He thought of the large medical bills run up in a vain effort to save the youngster's life and the impossibility of ever meeting these obligations on his $58-a-week salary. He thought of the food he sometimes could not buy for his wife and two other children.

And then Patrolman William Perry turned thief.

He took the cash box containing $282 from the counter of the store where he had checked a door early a day before and found it open. He hid the money under a pile of boxes outside and notified Police Chief William E. Gardiner a burglary had been committed.

Chief Gardiner took over from there and Perry went out again on

---

23. This appears to be Brown's take on an actual news account, as L. Francis Callan (not Callahan) was a judge in Middleboro, MA, in 1960.

patrol. The chief soon found the cash box and settled down to wait for a thief. He nabbed Perry when he returned a few hours later.

In court, District Judge L. Francis Callahan listened to Perry admit the theft. He was told Perry had resigned from the force.

But after listening to the entire story, the judge refused to accept a plea and waived the official reading of the complaint. Perry walked out of court a free man.

"There is no doubt he did this in a state of desperation," the judge said. "If it were not for the Grace of God we might have been in the same position."

THE LIGHTS
MARCH 30, 1960

More than anything, it was the puzzle of the two small lights that flashed from the near darkness of the pit of the Mexican cave that attracted the two young vacationers from New York. The sound of Bird still rang in their ears from the tape recorder they'd played in the hacienda last night. They hummed "Klactoveedsedstene"[24] as they glanced beyond the lip of the cave. The sand and rock below was partially blocked from view by a low hanging cloud. The town, a day's walk away was toy-like and minuscule.

"They pull you, don't they?"

"The lights?"

"Yeah, the lights. I'm going down. You hold the rope."

"It's pretty far."

"I got to know about those lights. You know what I mean?"

"Yeah. I'll hold the rope."

The descent was quick; sulphur and moisture grew thick as Rudell went down, circle by circle, toward the lights. Rope ran out, but still there was no bottom. He grew afraid.

"Dig, uh . . . like pull me up."

There was a tug at the rope. Another tug. And another.

"I can't, Rudy."

After the first fright. After the long passage of time when flesh gave way to fiber, and the muscles gave it all up, Rudell screamed, and fell.

---

24. A 1947 song by Charlie Parker.

He fell near the bare outline of what was once a man, now skeleton. He gasped once, turned his head toward the light. Spasmed, touched the light which the bones of the skeleton had once clutched. He clutched and squinted. The lights were the luminescent eyes of Jesus Christ upon a large wooden cross. He tried to laugh. He couldn't.

He died three hours later—clutching the cross.

BIRD LIVES
APRIL 4, 1960

It was only when the rent was due or when he saw another friend's picture in the *Defender*, a former schoolmate's, or heard that another buddy had bought a two flat out Eighty-Ninth Street that he got to thinking about Bird. It was only then that the thinness of his arms, and the shortness of his fingers, and the thickness of his brain, and the heaviness of his skin, and the weight of his body seemed to anchor him to earth—prevented him from knowing the freedom inside his head that allowed him to dream—and fly up, out and away, from the winoes, rentmen, swingmen, bosses, foremen, and policemen that floated in and out of his life like dirty corks upon a filthy sea.

He wanted something, and before, the image of Bird sitting in some second floor in some big city, thinking up new songs, and finding new ways to say things to his soul, before, this image had given his arms the feather and fiber of a bird—before he'd sailed away. But not now. The man was dead. And with his corpse was buried Dadelus' wings. D, as he was called, strode past the Fifty-Eighth Street "L," down the alley, where there lay a brick, white, and soft. He looked around, saw no one looking, picked up the brick, and wrote in large letters, something that made the junkies and winoes and even serious people shiver. The sign on the wall proclaimed:

BIRD LIVES!

BIRD——POSSESSED
APRIL 5, 1960

The band was doing alright except for the young cat on alto who kept messing up the whole thing with those funny out of tune notes. The lead trumpet, a fellow who'd done four years in Count's Kansas City band, was beginning to complain about the out-of-tune alto man.

"I don't think he's high. I think he's out of sight. If you want to keep that cat, I'm gonna have to cop me another gig. Really, the stud can't read music, and he can't blow. I don't know why you hired him."

The band leader hunched his shoulders and [said],[25]

"Like give the boy a break. I'll tell him to blow in tune. If he doesn't straighten up in a week, like later. Cool?"

"Tough. I go for that."

They gave the young out-of-tune alto man a week to straighten up. Instead of straightening up, he came in one night playing something that sounded like he was really into some other stuff.

"'Listen, Ornette. I hate to nut on you, baby, but the boys want to play for the people, and you want to play for the man in the moon. I got nothing against you, and I'll give you good references . . . dig?"

Ornette left. He applied for unemployment compensation the next day. And while waiting for the check to come in, he sat down and wrote out some more stuff that was even more weird than that which he'd gotten fired for.

One day a feather drifted through his window, and landed upon his shoulder. He smiled, and mumbled, "Bird."

MYSTERIOSIO
APRIL 7, 1960

Two by two they marched in. Black hoods covered their heads; their bodies were shrouded in robes black. A tone sounded. The after-sound of the tone resounded. And the Black Hoods held torches. Yellow curled from the flame of the torches and heat rippled the sight of every stone of the cave down which they marched. Down, down they marched.

---

25. This sentence was cut off, but this seems like the most likely missing text.

"Woe be unto he who tells of this fellowship. Woe to his soul and to his kin. Woe to he who speaks of what he sees here or does here, for surely vengeance and no mercy shall follow him all the days of his life . . ."

And the tone embellished the tone of his voice with a special gong quality.

Men talked. Hands were raised. Head nodded in agreement. Guns were passed. Bombs were passed. Keys to great mansions, warehouses, jails, powerhouses, capitol-halls, stores, schools and churches were passed.

"Woe be unto him who tells what he sees here."

Two by two the hooded figures marched upward to the ground's surface. Day came. No track, dropped paper, cigarette butt, cartridge, or march stick spoke of what had happened during the night. Nor did anyone speak. Neither did white; nor Negro. A bird did sing.

THE BENEDICTION[26]
APRIL 6, 1960

The feeling of God sometimes sets in a man and he must move in his soul or with his body as a flower moves to the light of the sun—he must move to the source of this feeling and sometimes it kills him. Sometimes he doesn't care. Sometimes he . . .

It started with an alto horn, and a young boy who'd grown faster than he should have, and who'd become great before he should have, and who sought for the source of the feeling deep inside before he should have. He stood in his room and started with a short burst of notes, and then sought the tone he'd felt inside him, but which he couldn't match, he couldn't match by blowing. He blew, fast, and beautifully; seeking the right burst of notes, notes blown so fast that only God's perfection would be a match for it. He tried for a tone that he'd never heard, but which he knew as a sensation of mystery, or greatness, a feeling that he was bigger than he seemed to be, could blow faster than his fingers were letting him, could cry out the tone that cried within him. All this strained inside him, strained and drove him, pushed him and made him whip his fingers upon the valves of his horn until they hurt. And

____

26. Unsigned.

his lungs seemed to bleed inside; his eyes ran water, and he kept blowing, and blowing, with his eyes closed to the white of the daytime and the touch of the wind and the sound of the fists banging at the door, and the bark of the voices outside his door, shouting: "Open up! It's the police! What's going on in there?"

DISTANT COUSINS
APRIL 13, 1960

The African was very dark, and his chest barreled above his belt over a big stomach that bulged beneath his ill-fitting American double breasted suit. His shirt was dirty around the collar and his face seemed scarred as though he'd been on the wrong side of a bad car wreck.

He sat in the car beside an American Negro whom he'd met at a meeting. The Negro drove his late model car with assurance, and an urbanity that seemed to the African exaggerated when compared to the way he'd seen other Negroes drive a car.

"What do you think of us, Nwankwo?"

The African smiled. The question had been asked many times.

"I think you are to be pitied."

"I thought you did, but look at us; I'm not 'free,' but then again I'm not worried about starving, and I've got a few things ... a car, some decent clothes. I ..."

"You're a slave to a color that is not your own. A slave to the heritage of Greece and Rome, not Ghana, or Dahomey. You've come from home, but you can't, as your great American white novelist, Thomas Wolfe, once said, 'go home again.' I ... I'm sorry ... I didn't mean to hurt your feelings."

"It ... it's alright ... I asked for it."

That night the American dreamed about drums.

PRIDE I
APRIL 20, 1960

"Is that the way you feel about it?"

(Please say something that will let me say that I'm sorry, that I love you.)

"What do you mean 'Is that the way I feel'? You're the one who started this."

(Oh Ronald, I don't want to be this way. Say something that will stop this.)

"Well, I guess it's good we found out how we feel about each other before we got married. I'm not going to run after you. I'll tell you that."

(Theresa, 1 don't want to lose you. What can I do? Please smile at me.)

"I'd say you were a hundred percent right, Ronald. I guess I'd better give you your ring back."

(Don't take it.)

"If that's the way you feel about it, I guess so."

(No!)

"Here you are, Ronald."

"Goodbye, Theresa."

"Goodbye, Ronald."

PRIDE II
APRIL 21, 1960

She laughed. It seemed funny to think that it had come to this. She was actually hungry, and there was not a piece of meat or a slice of fresh bread in the house. Old age pensions don't last a whole month: and . . . well, that's all there was to it, there was no food.

It was noon, and she'd always liked a bit of cheese and soft bread at noon. Maybe a cup of coffee. She thought about going to the phone (her son insisted that she let him take care of the phone bill), and calling him. Two dollars, she thought, would do it. But no, she decided, she'd wait.

Evening took a long time getting there, but it came, and now her stomach was beginning to hurt. All kidding aside, she thought as she sat in the second floor window watching the kids go by eating candy bars, munching hamburgers, and licking popsicles, maybe I'd better call Richard. But she'd never been really hungry before. She'd always had Daddy when she'd asked Richard for money before. She'd never really needed it.

She started downstairs, went into the drugstore, dialed WR 2-3330. The phone rang, someone on the other end said:

"Hello?"
She couldn't answer.
"Hello?"
She wouldn't answer.
She slowly hung up. She headed back upstairs. She could not do it. She decided she'd wait a little longer, until she was just a little hungrier.

PRIDE III
APRIL 27, 1960

If he'd been twenty, he would have killed her. But being five years old, he had to duck low. He was, "in the wind," as it were. And it had started so innocently too. Really. Like,
"Here's a cookie honey."
And like he took it, and started out of the kitchen.
"Aren't you going to say thanks?"
What was it? The tone of her voice? The fact that he didn't know why he should have to say two "things" to his own mother just for giving him a sweet? And anyway what was "thanks?"
He smiled at her, but said nothing.
"Say thanks!"
She snatched the cookie out of his hand.
He said nothing.
"Say thanks! Say it!"
She shook him.
"Say thanks!"
Nothing.
She gave him the cookie. He started to eat it. She took it away from him just before it reached his mouth.
"Say thanks."
He started to cry. She gave him the cookie again, and took it away again.
"Say it!"
She shook him. She slapped his face.
He said nothing. Now, he'd say nothing, not even if she killed him.

FEAR I
MAY 2, 1960

We were wet, and we stunk. The mud was "eastern mud." Sticky, hot, clutching South Pacific mud. We marched, the five of us, single file. And the slush-slup, slush-slup of our feet plunging into and straining out of the goo, made the mission seem nasty. We were going to raid a Korean village. There were, we'd been told, some "gooks" there. We were going to destroy that village. We had to. The "gooks" had been raiding our outposts. "Big Kiddy from New Yawk City" had been killed last night. Throat cut. That was why I volunteered to go. I liked "Big Kiddy."

A young boy in front of me was letting the other guys get too far ahead of him. I didn't tell him to move faster. I knew what his slowness meant. I knew he would panic. I knew he would die . . . running the other way. I prepared myself for it.

It came. We reached the village. One light burned in a grass and stick hut and the turgid water of a swamp picked up the light, and flashed it on the metal of some ten or twelve "gooks" flat-bellied around the swamp, whispering, lounging and sleeping.

Something moved behind me. Something moved in front of me, and on the side of me. I figured that it was a wind. I tensed. The boy in front of me figured, I guess, that it was a trap. He shouldered his carbine, stopped spreadlegged, and whimpering. I heard the safety go off and I hit the dust. I tried to pull the boy down with me, but it was too late. He fired at the sound around us, and light from the trees above us cut him down and strafed for the rest of us.

FEAR II
MAY 3, 1960

Her mother came out of the bedroom just as he started to pick his teeth. He poked, licked, swallowed, licked his lips again, slid down on the couch, stared at the shined tip of his shoes, crossed his legs, looked up at Mrs. Jenkins and smiled.

"Hello, Mizzus Jenkins."

"Hello, Harmon. Katherine'll be here in a minute."

"Oh, that's alright Mizzus Jenkins."

He picked at his teeth again, belched without saying "excuse me," eased his hand into the pocket of his tight-fitting pure silk continental style slacks, and pulled out something which escaped Mrs. Jenkins' glance, for she'd been distracted at that moment by the stubby form of a rat strolling across the floor on its way to the kitchen. She shuddered, looked around for a broom with which to chase the rat, and seeing no broom, smiled at the processed-haired, smooth face, smiling tooth picking twenty three year old beau of her daughter aslouch on her couch.

"I brought something for Katherine, Mizzus Jenkins."

He opened his hand and the glint of diamond took the room's light to itself and sprayed against the somber walls of the shadowy room, flashed against the dusty picture of a dead husband, slanted and forgotten against the far wall.

"I'm gonnn as' her to marry me, Mizzus Jenkins. Is it okay?"

Olivia Jenkins, widow, age 50, part time clerk at North Center Department Store, daughter 20, tenant of 4100 South Berkeley, third floor rear, five rings, stared at the kitchen into which the rat had strolled, stared at the room from which her daughter would come, stared at the conk-head waiting on the couch, stared into the kitchen, and beyond it to the greasy, toilet-smelling future, and smiled and swallowed, and forced the tears back down her throat and said:

"Why honey, you know it is."

FEAR III
MAY 4, 1960

He was nearly through reading, and it made him nervous to be almost through reading. Even as he read the last words of the last page of the book he started thinking about what other books he could read. He thought of one just as he finished the last page. He held the finished book in his hands and walked to his father's book rack in the basement. He picked a pocket book out of a row of books; it was *Crime and Punishment* by Fyodor Dostoevsky. He started the story. He suffered with Raskolnikov when he killed the woman. He felt the fear Raskolnikov felt when he ran into the streets, and to his room. He had hot spells when the main character had fever. He cried when R. kissed the feet of his meek, mild sweetheart.

He finished the book with tears in his eyes when R. turned himself in as the murderer of the old woman. He quickly found another book and another, and another, and suddenly one day he was thirty. He went back into his books and read Wells' *Outline of History* and John Stuart Mill's *On Liberty* and the Bible, and Marx' *Capital*, and the magazines, *Time, Life, Look, Foreign Affairs*, and the Bible again, and *Capital* again. And he looked up again and this time he was sixty. He went down again and read Sophocles, Herodotus, Epictetus, Homer, Aristotle, and Euripides, and this time when he read *Look, Foreign Affairs*, and the Bible again, stopped reading; he'd done it. He'd made it through life without looking. He was smiling the morning he died.

FEAR IV
MAY 5, 1960

"So what kind of woman do you think I am?"

"What do you mean? I just asked you if you would like . . ."

"I know what you asked me. And I say again, what kind of . . ."

"I heard you the first time. If you're going to be so nasty about it, then forget it. There are more widows than you to take out."

"Well, just a minute, I didn't say I wouldn't go out with you. I just didn't like the way you asked me. 'Hey babe, how about a date.' What kind of way is that to talk to a woman?"

"Well, I didn't mean to make you so mad. I guess I shouldn't have asked you. So, forget it."

"Where would you have taken me if I had said yes?"

"What does it matter?"

"Well, a woman likes to go out sometimes."

"She does?"

"Sure she does. Uh . . . how about a . . ."

"A what?"

"A . . ."

"A what?"

"I'd appreciate very much going out with you, Fred."

PRIDE IV
MAY 7, 1960

Darkness and light, darkness and light, it alternated with the moon's fogged bright. And over the country plain, with the scent of the rain, and the smell of cut grass and hay, he came. Speeding through mist and the night lonely plain down a single lane, country, bumpy, evening lane after a rain, he came, heading home, alone.

His headlights drove the darkness before him, herding it ahead, as sheep by a dog, pressing and flowing into the clouds hung low, and caught in the branches and bark, the dark trees' bark, cloud tufted in the dark. He saw the light of the car just ahead, saw it and dimmed his light to acknowledge. The lane was small and the car just ahead, headed toward him as though its driver were dead. Its dark, sleeping driver were dead.

He flashed his lights, at the oncoming light but the light kept coming till it was just ahead. Something in him locked his foot to the gas. He decided that he would not be the first one to pass. He'd not swerve to the edge of the country black road. This the other must do. He decided to be bold. He was bold, it was told, to the coroner jury that he drove like a fury down the dark one-lane road. Some "thing" had taken hold, the jury was told. He'd crashed on a "tree" brightly adorned with round, reflecting tin "eyes" just off of the road.

FEAR V
MAY 9, 1960

It was just a tie pin, he thought. Anybody could have left it. Why should I get so excited about a little tie pin. But then again he thought, how about that mysterious phone call? And why did the party hang up when I answered the phone?

The ten o'clock rest period bell rang. He went to the locker room, sat on the bench, away from the rest of the guys. He thought and thought. The bell rang again, and he went back to work.

And she sure was acting funny last night. I noticed a lot of coolness in her. I wonder if she didn't feel so hot like she said. And why didn't she feel so hot? I wonder if they had a quarrel, her and her mysterious phone call. I bet he's there right now. I bet he's there and he's . . .

Billy Jo cut off his machine. He went to his foreman. He fixed his face in a real sick expression, and said,

"Sam, I feel sick as the devil. I think I'll go home?"

"Now?"

"Right this minute."

HISTORY I
MAY 10, 1960

"Momma, what did your mother look like?"

"My mother was a beautiful woman. She had long black hair. She looked like an Indian. She used to make me cookies, and braid my hair in long Indian braids. I used to have real long hair, that is until the first time I went to the beauty shop and that silly woman burned it all out."

"What did your father look like?"

"My father? Oh, he was tall, and kind of brownskinned, and he had wavy hair, and big broad shoulders. He always had money in his pocket. And he used to take me with him to see his friends. Oh, I remember one time we were . . ."

"Why are you crying, Momma?"

"I'm not crying."

"I see tears on your face."

"I'm not crying!"

"Momma?"

"What do you want?"

"What did daddy look like?"

HISTORY II
MAY 11, 1960

"Why, what you say. Back a few years, when I was home, shucks! Why we used to live ten times better than we do up here right now. Now let me tell you. Sure they didn't like you down there, but boy, what you say! A man knew where he stood. Up here they two faced. Tell you you're free and you can do anything you want to, but then they pull the same old thing on you, only in a sneaky way. Why, my ol' boss, mista MacAdoo, what you say. When cotton choppin' time is over, why he'd give us a big slaba fat back, and two hunnut pound sacksa yella cone mill and a few clothes for the chilluns and, what you say. Boy, we didn't have all this innagration, and trouble and all like that."

A voice came over the ballpark's loudspeaker.

"And now, our National Anthem."

The great band started to play, and the baritone led the singing. Thomas Burton stood, and raised his face to the flag near home plate. He sang loud and clear,

". . . and the rockits red glauh. The bombs bustin' in ahr . . ."

When the song ended, Mr. Burton sat down, and continued talking,

"Only one time I seen a boy git shot by some white folks, and that was his fault. He was goin with one a them fast white gals in town and they caught up with him."

His companion, a man some five years his junior, took out a cigarette, lit it and took a long, long drag. He tried to fill his heart, lungs, and brain with smoke so that he would not be able to hear any more history.

THE NEW JOB
MAY 17, 1960

Now why they were going to kill him I don't know. Perhaps he didn't pay somebody some money he owed them, or maybe it was somebody's husband who figured that this was the best way to break up an unpleasant affair. Anyway, they knew that he stepped off the Jackson Park "L" at Fifty-Fifth Street at 10:05 every night, and they knew too that he cut along the gangway beside the station and went home by way of Fifty-Fifth Place.

And so they waited. Sure enough he came at his regular time, and they followed him, and according to plan one crossed the street in case he should run that way, while the other stayed behind him.

He was just whistling and going on when the one behind him tapped his shoulder, and drew back to unhead him. He didn't waste motions, he whipped out a big Magnum, and boomed the would-be murderer to the walk.

The other man ran. The next day, after his reports were filed and all, his commanding officer said,

"To have just been made a policeman, I must say you sure got off to a fine start."

HISTORY III
MAY 18, 1960

The police blocked both ends of the block. All four of them got out at the end of Fifty-Eighth Street, and the other squad started to slow crawl down Calumet toward the building where Calvin Smith was trapped.

"Car 120, car 120, over to Fifty-Eighth and Calumet; dangerous man with gun. Cars 200, 321, 416, and 512 ditto, over."

Soon all cars were there. The red lights were flashing, and policemen were pushing people away from the building where they had Calvin Smith trapped.

"There he is!" a policeman shouted, and as he did, another policeman in plainclothes called to two men standing near the door.

"Go get him, boys."

The two men eased, in a single smooth motion, their guns from their hips and swept through the double hall doors, and up the stairs.

Again the head peered from the third floor window. A shot rang. The head disappeared. Another shot rang, and another. Then silence.

More cars appeared, more men in plainclothes. Once more someone shouted,

"Look, he's on the roof."

Another shot.

Minutes passed. Five men, including the two who had first rushed in, came out of the building. There was a stiffness about their faces.

Someone asked,

"Did you get him?"

One of them muttered,

"The . . . got away."

A woman in the crowd laughed. A young boy said,

"Did you see that cat leap over them roofs? Man, he was great."

CAUSE OF IT ALL
MAY 19, 1960

It was the same thing every time he saw her. There was nothing that she said or did. Yet it was there, and there was nothing he could do about it until it happened. He knew it, that's all. He just knew it.

It wasn't long before he'd have to speak to her. One doesn't go into the record shop every Saturday and not speak to a beautiful woman sooner or later.

"May I see that record?"

It was not the way he thought it would be, and anyhow, here it was. He handed her the record without saying anything. She read it, and smiled, and handed it back to him.

"I like Thelonious Monk. They say that women aren't supposed to like his music, too modern or something; I don't know, but I like him."

What else was there for him to say, but,

"Would you like to listen to it with me!"

"Yes, I think I would."

They went into the booth, played the record, agreed that it was one of Monk's best pieces in years. He bought the record, and started out. She bought a record and walked out beside him. They stepped onto the sidewalk in front of the walk, and turned to each other to say goodbye, when a man pulled his car alongside the curb, and cursing, and crying, and charging toward them, pulled out a gun, and shot him. He fell; the pain spread through his chest. He wondered, just before he died, how he knew that she would be the cause of it all.

"BYYYEE. . ."
MAY 23, 1960

Talk about a cat running, Jim, this stud was making it. Down South Parkway to Fifty-Fifth; over Garfield Boulevard to Prairie, past Indiana to Michigan. I'm telling you he was cutting! And all the time he was mumbling to himself,

"Eighteen minutes," and a little later, "seventeen minutes," and, "sixteen minutes," and so on.

Running and sweating. He was almost there when a man grabbed his arm, and said,

"Hey Cool Daddy, I seen your woman last night. She said to tell you . . ."

"Don't stop me man. Baby Blue's going to get my hi-fi out of pawn if I don't redeem it in . . ."

He caught the clock at Fifty-Fifth and Michigan.

"Good Gordon's gin! I got one minute. That stud's gon' sell my hi-fi to Baby Blue if I'm not there by three, and it's two fifty-nine. Dig baby, I gotta split."

And he did. He was almost there when a policeman called.

"Hey you, there. Hold it."

"Officer I can't . . . I gotta . . ."

"I said hold it."

He held it. The officer searched him. Looked at his arms, and let him go.

He got there just in time to see Baby Blue walking out with a neat mahogany hi-fidelity set with the word Magnavox beautifully engraved on the side.

Baby Blue said,

"Byyyyyree . . ."

HOLIDAY
JUNE 16, 1960
SHORT, SHORT STORY

"Into the black box they will go, the tall and the long ones and the fat kings and consuls, into the box and the long ride they will take and they will smile at the satin tops of closed places, and evening will be with them always, and no sound save the burrowing noise of hungry things below, should greet their ears—shall eat their ears.

"Say something you big, lanky, four eyed thing, standing on your open top Fleetwood, riding down Fifth Avenue, or Pennsylvania! Say a word about how you intend to issue an order to the worms, and dictate a letter to be sent by cable to the beetles and grass roots, and oak roots."

The writing was going good for Little Dan. He lived in Altgeld and on Sundays, he went over to the edge of the thick river that rounded the island upon which the Acme Steel Mill[27] stood smoking.

"And now you see that heaven was where you were, my man. And now you see that sleep is a long thing, a lonesome trip with no passing trees or poles to mark off minutes or centuries . . ."

A policeman on a three-wheel slowed up and eyed him. He smiled. The policeman didn't smile. He stood and brushed himself off, and looked at his paper, read it once, crumpled it and threw it into the water. Some buddies came by, he hitched a ride back to Altgeld. There was a fight going on on the corner. He stopped to watch it . . . anything to keep from going home.

INSANITY
JUNE 22, 1960
SHORT, SHORT STORY

The psychologist was at last inside a Negro mind. It was for the first time. He felt sick.

"To belong is important," said the pages of the book the psychologist had read as he thought about the mind he'd just gaped down into.

Here he saw a man at the rear of a bus stop lunch room, eating greasy chicken from a paper plate.

"Every human being needs a sense of security." This is the book talking! "He needs to know that he will be alive the next day, that his hunger and shelter needs are provided for, or that there is a chance of their being provided for. Without this assurance, the human being becomes disorganized, disoriented and hostile to those he deems responsible for his lack of security. He . . ."

The psychologist remembered the talk of his patient's early childhood—the moving from room to kitchenette, to hotel, to rat sieged room. He remembered the talk about relief, and case workers, and night time investigators, and the patient's father hiding under the bed.

"Violence is a reaction to frustration . . . murder and suicide often reflect a state of complete emotional disintegration . . ."

The psychologist called his secretary,

------

27. Altgeld Gardens is a Chicago Public Housing development along the Little Calumet River on the far south side of Chicago. The Acme Steel Mill was just north of Altgeld in what is now Big Marsh Park.

"Miss Jones, take a letter. Ready? Okay. Here it is. I, Doctor Vladimir Zoo, hereby declare that the accused should be found not guilty by reason of . . ."

WANTS SOMETHING
JUNE 23, 1960
SHORT, SHORT STORY

I know what he wanted. I'll tell you that right now. He wanted some rules, something to go by. You know what I mean? He was afraid that if something or somebody wasn't always keeping him heading this way, or that way, why, he'd fall right off the edge of the world.

Don't laugh, you're probably just as bad. I know I am. Anyway, needing these rules and all is what got him in trouble. In the first place, he never should have taken a chance on that Irish Sweepstake ticket. But how can you tell a guy like that something?

In the second place, he never should have let the man keep both tickets. It seems the man was in a hurry, and he couldn't get the receipt out, and so he read off the number of the ticket to Raymous and Raymous wrote it down, and forgot about it until he saw the number in the paper. Then he went to the man who sold him the ticket and asked for the money. Let's see, how much was it? Two or three hundred thousand dollars.

"Man, you didn't buy no ticket from me!"

When like I said, the kid needed rules to go by. All his life he went by rules, but there was no rule for this kind of deal. So you know what? Raymous shot the stud—five times. Well, he went up the way for seventy-five years, but he's a stepper and I'm sure he'll come out alright, but if only he had had a rule for a situation like that sweepstake bit. Why, I'll bet he'd be making the "set" right now!

THE DIME
JULY 6, 1960

"Dig, baby. I don't want to bug you, but I got to have a dime a day. I mean like my short is behind on the payments and the man is on me."

"A dime! I don't make but twenty cents myself. You know you haven't been digging up no Rockefellers."

"I know what I've been doing, scrounge. I'm not asking you. I'm telling you. I gotta have a dime a day."

"Look Homer, honey . . . I . . . I need that bread. I told you when I first started to . . . well, when everything started that I was only doing this to take care of my husband. He's sick and we need doctor money, and food money, and . . ."

"Look don't try to cop on me. I'm not playing with you. I will mess you up! I want that bread. If you keep on, I'll just go to your old man and scream on you. I mean like the whole bit. Dig?"

"I'll kill you."

"Cool."

"Okay . . ."

"Okay what?"

"Okay, I'll . . . give . . . I'll give you the extra ten dollars."

"Crazy."

"You dirty . . ."

YOCKY DOCK[28]
JULY 7, 1960

The truth is . . . that wine just wouldn't let ol' Yocky Dock go. Snow piled up on him and the pile of newspaper near the Fifty-Eighth Street "L" where he had staggered and fallen. He pushed himself up on his elbow and took some matches from his back pocket. There were two left. He lit one of the matches and tried to stick it to the paper, but the wind blew the match out just before the paper lit up.

Yocky tried to move his feet, but wasn't nothing happening. Yocky was getting sleepy, but he was too hip for that. He knew from the movies they used to show at the N.R.A.[29] that if you went to sleep in the cold, you would die.

He looked at the match packet. One match left. Yocky started saying, "Our Father who art in heaven . . ." but he could not remember the

---

28. Unsigned.

29. Perhaps the National Recovery Administration, a New Deal program that ran from 1933 to 1935.

rest of it and so he lit the match. He stuck it to the paper; the paper started burning. Yocky started to crying and laughing. He was glad that he didn't have to die.

The wind licked the fire right off of that paper. Yocky called the wind a bad word. He sat there for a while, staring at the "L" posts running down the dark alley, and thinking about his brother back in Topeka; then without realizing it, he dropped off to sleep.

POSSESSIVE
JULY 11, 1960

It wasn't anything except that she was an hour late getting home, and the seam of her stocking was turned inside out.

"The traffic was pretty heavy today, huh baby?"

"Yes, it was."

"This is the second time this week that traffic has been heavy."

"Are you testing me, Tony?"

He did not answer. This reply hurt him. He sat there frowning. Then he remembered Ed Taylor. The nice neighbor who'd taken Mae to work once last winter. Ed had passed the house, about ten minutes before Mae had come home.

"I can't believe it."

"You can't believe what, Tony?"

He didn't answer. He thought about his bald head and his fat stomach.

"Ed Taylor is a pretty nice looking guy, isn't he?"

"Why do you mention him?"

"Can't you stand to hear me call his name, Mae?"

He hated himself for sinking to this . . . this prying. But he hated her for making him feel this way. He glared at her. She looked at him with surprise.

"I ought to kick your teeth out."

"You what?"

He hit her. It was the first time he'd ever done a thing like that in his life.

MOHOLO
JULY 13, 1960

A female panther screamed somewhere behind the bush beyond the compound. It was dark. The night had a moon, but clouds had hidden it, and so the jungle was grey. Light seemed to come from no special place. Everything was grey.

An orange blaze wavered on the side of a hill not too far from Moholo's hut. The sweat under his armpits ran along his sides, and he scratched his neck even though it didn't itch.

There was another scream. Moholo bit his lip. Kulao was dying, he thought. Now they were cutting his stomach. It was always the last thing they did. It was always the thing that made a man scream off the hill above the scream of the wind and the pregnant panthers.

Moholo turned away from the opening at his hut's wall, away from the fire and the screams. He stared at the slow breathing forms of Dalca, his wife, and Tall Spear, his nickname for his son. He hit his face with his fist, and cried out. No one heard him.

He walked to the door, stopped and walked to his wife and child. Then he walked to the opening. It would be so easy to run away, but the Kikuyu elders would order the death of these sleeping two. They would die because of what he'd done. Umtadah had given him money just for telling where the Mau were meeting. It was good, the money. It bought cloth for the woman, and a sweet for the boy. Now they were cutting Umtadah's stomach. He would tell. And soon they'd be after him. Again he walked to his wife and son, but again he stopped. How far would they get? What about the panthers? What about the fleet-footed young warriors of the camp?

Again the panther screamed. The fire on the hill went out. Moholo bit his lip. They were coming.

THE COOL ONE
JULY 14, 1960

He looked at her, and frowned. Something about his youngest daughter, the third girl, just disgusted him. The oldest girl was a brain, nothing but doubles, and prizes in school. The middle girl was no brain, but she could charm you right out of your socks, he thought. But this one . . .

"Daddy, where are you going?"

"To the garage to get my spare tire fixed."

"Can I go?"

Oh boy! What did I tell you?

"Ooookay . . . come on."

So they went and she waited in the car while he attended to business.

Five minutes later, the young daughter came into the station. He looked at her. Frowned.

"So what do you want. I told you not to bother me. I shouldn't have brought you in the first place. What do you . . ."

"Daddy," she was TOO cool, "the car is moving."

He rushed out of the station. The car was rolling down a slight hill into the street, toward the canyon workmen had dug for the Southside Expressway.[30] He leaped into the car and slammed on the brakes, wiped his forehead, and sat there thinking. The child had been smart enough to get out of the car. She had come to tell him. She had even closed the door behind her. And she WAS cool. He smiled at her as she came to the car, and got in. He hugged her. He gave her a quarter. He gave her another quarter. He hugged her again.

But nothing he did seemed to be enough to express what he felt.

THE WITNESS I
JULY 25, 1960

Now you take me for example. I'm seventeen, but do you think anybody cares about this? You'd better believe it. I mean like they don't. You dig? Really. 'Cause like the other night I was laying there trying to go to sleep. That simple history teacher had threatened to give an exam the next day; the dance was Friday night and I didn't have a decent pair of shoes nowhere in sight, and my only cuffless was dirty and I didn't have nothing looking like cleaning money. And asking dad for it was too piercing. I mean I'd rather skip the dance behind having to go through all that, "You ought to have a job, why when I was your age I was supporting my . . ." bit. So I didn't even

---

30 The Dan Ryan Expressway, which opened in 1961.

think about asking him. And well, to tell you the truth, I had hyped momma so much lately that I didn't have nerve to ask her for anything else.

So on top of all this worry, they starts all that...well, that, what shall I say? I mean I'm seventeen alright and all that, but...damn! I'm human too, and well, after all they are my own mother and father. I mean like twelve o'clock? What's wrong with one or two...I mean I just might not have been asleep you know? Oh, don't tell me about being grownup and all that jazz. I didn't buy this house. And I sure didn't ask for walls like these. Oh well, I just won't think about it. Now let me see...If I borrow a quarter from Buggy, and a dime from Duck, that'll be thirty-five cents and...

THE WITNESS II
JULY 26, 1960

Ohhh, this jive, jive broad. All this doggone noise and commotion. Like I'm suppose to be a fool or something. Don't she think I know what's happening? Shopping Monday, Tuesday, Wednesday evenings and the stores aren't even open late on Tuesday and Wednesday evenings. "I stopped by to see Aunt Mary, honey...I dropped in the beauty shop, baby...I stopped to get the car washed, sweetheart ..." Now dig her, ain't this some...stuff. I ought to get up and bust her cap.

And that overgrown boy in there. What's he on his bottom about? Don't half speak. And always begging me for money. What am I supposed to be, Reverend Roddie or somebody! Ohhh, woman stop that noise!

"Huh, baby? Oh yes, I do."

Boy, oh boy. I ought to give her an Academy Award for acting. What am I going to do? I don't want to have her riding me for alimony. It's cheaper to stay here. But if she ONLY STOP THAT...NOISE!

"Huh, baby? Oh yes, I do."

THE WITNESS III
JULY 27, 1960

Ho hum...one two three...cha, cha, cha. Why oh why didn't I take that old cat up on his offer. A Mark V, a home in Chatham, money in the bank, and him ninety years old. Now look...just look at this fat bas...ketball stomach looking thing. And he used to look so nice too. A regular young man in a hurry. Going to be somebody someday. Well, at least I've got Billy, but God, he's seventeen, and he'll be leaving any day himself. And then what will 1 have?

"Charles, do you love me?"

Plus he's slowed down considerable. Been messing around with too many of those young foxes. And has nerve to ask me about shopping too much in the evenings. It would be different if I was into something, but I'm not. I wonder if Billy's asleep. He must be. It's twelve o'clock. Oh God, what am I going to do?

"Charles, do you love me?"

THE WITNESS IV
JULY 28, 1960

I wonder if these idiots don't know that a parakeet got good sense. These are the dumbest people I ever saw to be human beings. Daddy-O Daylie[31] sure said it when he started calling them jive cats. These sure are some jive studs. I've been in this damn cage for ten years and they haven't had sense enough to put a cover over since I've been here.

Listen to her! "Charles do you love me? Charles do you love me?" And talk about the stud like a dog when he's gone. Boy, I wouldn't be a human for all the pod in China. And that bull dog face looking Billy. If he sticks his filthy finger in this cage just one more time, I'll definger that...Boy, I'm getting to be as bad as they are. I never thought this way when I was in the pet shop. Holy eagles! Of all the people that could have bought me. I had to be bought by THESE jive people.

---

31. Holmes "Daddy-O" Daylie was a radio DJ who was the first to play jazz and be-bop on Chicago radio stations.

And ole Charlie sure thinks he's slick, hiding money in my water cup wrapped in wax paper. I sure wish my bill was as strong as it used to be. I'd mess with him good!

Oh, there she goes again, "Charlie, do you love me?"

Oh, somebody get me outa here!

THE CONFORMIST
AUGUST 2, 1960

He glimpsed at the McKie Fitzhugh[32] dance poster as he ran. GENE AMMONS, GENE WRIGHT AND THE DUKES OF SWING, it said. That sign was from nineteen forty something and other signs were tacked on to it but they had peeled away and so it was this sign that stuck in his mind as he ran.

"Catch him! There he goes! Halt! We're police officers!"

He ducked underneath the legs of a fat brown horse dragging a wagon loaded with watermelons and young boys shouting, "Eeeyo-aayy, git yo red ripe watomilons he-uh!"

Sounds of teeth chomping the sweet juicy pap of red and dripping melons on the back porch at 47th and Calumet, with the cool air blowing between toes of feet propped on the sagging banisters of the grey back porches rush around his ears. Sounds of "L" trains and high heels rushing from the platform to the trains haunted his inner world as a bullet from the outer world romped from the officer's revolver and ripped into his back and rapped his brain and rocked him like a wobbling milk bottle about to fall.

Just one more memory. Just one more. He got up and gripped the wagon's wheels and lifted his eye to the sky, but a big neon sign hung between him and the sky, and it kept winking at him. There was some writing on the sign. It said,

DRINK GUZZLE BEER AND YOU'LL FEEL LIKE A ... and ... but then another bullet hit him so he couldn't finish reading the sign.

---

32. The owner of McKie's Disk Jockey Lounge.

A NICE BOY
AUGUST 3, 1960

"Is here alright?"

She looked at the grass, and at the drooping willow trees nearby and said,

"Uh huh. Let's sit here."

He spread the newspaper he'd bought at Blount's and they sat side by side.

"Uh, were you kidding when you said you liked me?"

She smiled at the tips of her shoes. She couldn't look at him. She answered softly,

"Did you mean it when you said you liked me?"

"Yes, I meant it."

"Well, I did too then."

"Suppose I'd said no."

"Then I would have said no too."

He put his arm around her. She moved his arm.

"What's the matter? I thought you liked me!"

"I do, but that doesn't mean that you have to do all that. If you want to marry me, we'll get married, and then you can do all that, but not before."

He got up and started to fold his paper up. She sure was a funny style broad. He thought as he neatly folded the paper, if I don't get this paper too wrinkled maybe I can find Louise and bring her out here.

"'Scuse me. Will you get off of the paper?"

THE NEWS
AUGUST 11, 1960

How to tell him, how to tell him. She sat at the window waiting and wondering what to say when he came home from work. One baby was okay, two not bad, three, well . . . but four! She thought, I am into something. One o'clock came and went. Two, three, four . . . he'd be there at four thirty.

"Hi, honey. Did you have a hard day at work today?"

"Yeah. I spent all day talking to Thomas. That cat is all shook up."

"Why?"

"His wife is going to have a baby. Do you know this makes number four. That chick is something else. Boy, Thomas is 'bout out of his head. What's new with you?"

"Who, me?"

"Yes, you."

"Uh . . . nothin'. Nothing at all."

THE FIGHT
AUGUST 15, 1960

Sweat and gloves and the biting smell of resin ran in and out of his body, mind and nose as he waited in the dressing room for his turn to go into the ring.

His mind was on the time he was on Fifty-First and he'd run into a boy who had a big picture of Sugar Ray. Sugar had his hair done up nice and he had the pose and the sharp look of a real champ. The Joe Louis gym[33] was near and he stopped in and the next thing he knew he was training and punching the bag and sparring and punching the bag.

Now he was here, in the dressing room alone. Mackie had gone to see when they were going to call him. Alone and scared. He waited. The door opened, Mackie came in.

The door opened. There was no roar of the crowd. No beautiful girl waiting on the front row.

Just a few scattered chairs, a lot of smoke and a great big white boy waiting for him in the ring.

He took a deep breath and started walking toward the ring.

JAM SESSION
AUGUST 16, 1960

"Speedeeyahduweee! Uh sillyahdow Shabbadotta-doo-dee-dot."

Little Brother leaned on the parking meter while Baby Bird went through his changes. The little cat could wail. Everybody knew that.

---

33. The Joe Louis Gym, at 64 E. 51st St., was run by Louis's stepbrother Pat Brooks Jr.

But today he was really into something. His mouth was going a bar a second, and he had his eyes shut and his hands limp at his sides, and he was going!

Six or seven other guys were standing by. And they were gassed—'cause Little Brother was known throughout the neighborhood as the cat who if he could blow an instrument, could probably have blown Bird off the stage. So it was really something to wait and see what he was going to do when Baby Bird, the young got through. Now Baby Bird was making like John Coltrane.

"Aahhhhhoouuuu. Aahhhoodayyy. Aahhhoouuudayy. Sweebe-dee-bee-deebee-beeee."

Little Brother just couldn't wait. He broke in on Baby Bird with a real quiet Lester riff. And he moved in a funny coughing drum chorus, and then he started to sway and cough and sway and cough and then he just coughed and coughed.

He tasted something funny in his mouth.

He coughed it up.

It was blood.

Now he knew it was true. The doctor hadn't lied to him. He started crying and he ran home—crying.

WITH THE GAME
AUGUST 17, 1960

It lay on the bar—a twenty.

"Hey bartender! Bartender, give my baby another House of Lords."

The bartender steady poured. He smiled and bowed and Uncle Tommed up a breeze.

"Yessir. Right away."

She watched the bartender take the twenty away. He brought back eighteen dollars. She said,

"Isn't this drink a dollar and a half?"

The bartender smiled,

"Oh my goodness. It certainly is. I'm so sorry."

He put the fifty cents on the bar.

"Yessir bartender. That's my baby lookin' out for me. Give me another one on the rocks."

This time the change was seventeen dollars. The woman winced.

"Hey bartender, you're a nice guy. Here's five dollars. You got kids?"

"Oh yessir, yessir, yessir."

Twelve dollars. Things were getting bad. And didn't look like he had any more than that one twenty. The woman squirmed on the stool.

"Hey bartender, give us both another one. You want one too?"

"Oh yessir, yessir, yessir."

"Well take one for yourself! Right baby? Right?"

The woman counted up right quick...four fifty...seven fifty change. She picked the twelve dollars off the bar.

"Honey, I'll be back. I'm going to get you a package of cigarettes."

"You hear that bartender? Ain't she sweet?"

"Uh...yessir. She's real choice...really down with the game."

THE POOR LADY
AUGUST 22, 1960

The woman walked across the thick carpet carrying the full-sized mink over her arm.

"Is there anything else, ma'm?"

"No, that's all." She continued talking to her friend sitting beside her.

"And if you only knew how I suffered with that man. I'd go out to play bridge, and when I got back, there he'd be, asking me why I was getting in at daybreak. I'm telling you I nearly had a nervous break-down fooling around with that man. Listen, let me tell you. I'd send his clothes to the cleaners, his shirts to the laundry, order dinner from Stouffers for him every night, keep our bank accounts balanced. I never overdrew our checking account.

"Honey, and on top of that, he had nerve enough to tell me that he was tired of our using separate bedrooms. After I had him one built in the basement where he'd be away from noise and all. Girl, I'm telling you. If I'd known he would turn out to be like he was, I would have divorced him a long time ago. His money didn't impress me, not one little bit."

The clerk brought the mink back, beautifully boxed.

"Would you like to take it with, ma'm?"

"Take it? In August? Of course not. Send it to my home."

She continued talking to her friend as they left the salon.

"Now girl, you be sure to write me. Box 12, Mexico City, Mexico."

THE STEREO SET
AUGUST 24, 1960

Now don't start telling me about what I should have done. I told you once, I didn't hear that girl screaming. Aww, you a lie. I didn't want her to burn. I was running down the hallway carrying my stereo set, and I heard something making some kind of noise in Room 323. Everybody else was running and carrying out their most important things. Why shouldn't I? No, no, no! You don't understand. I told the fireman that I thought I heard some*thing* in that room, not some*one*. I couldn't stop to see. I would have had to put my stereo down. Listen baby, I put good bread for this stereophonic record player and combination radio. I wasn't about to put it down and stop and see if what I heard was some- body instead of just maybe a dog or something. I mean look. If you're saying that I value my stereo set more than I do a perfect stranger. Why I'd only seen Maybelle to speak to her. She didn't mean anything to me. But I did not . . . How did I know it was Maybelle screaming? Why I . . . well . . . now look here: are you saying I let Maybelle burn alive in that room on purpose?

JUST IN TIME
AUGUST 25, 1960

Everything smelled like smoke and sweat and policemen's thick blue uniforms. She bumped by the lawyers and defendants, past the tall polished doors with the judges' names over them. She was crying but not loud. Mainly she was out of breath. She mumbled,

"Doggoned Loopy, just now telling he's up for trial today . . . 'scuse me . . . 'scuse me . . . 'scuse me please!"

She found it. She started to go in. A bailiff grabbed her wrist.

"Are you a witness?""

"No, my son . . ."

"Are you a lawyer or a defendant?"

"I told you, mister, my son is . . ."

"I'm sorry, ma'm, the courtroom is all filled up. Can't nobody go in but . . ."

"Are you a fool? My son is on trial in there and you ain't gon' let me in to talk for him? Why you must be a fool. If you don't get outa my way I'll turn this place upside down!"

She pushed the bailiff and snatched the door open. She had just made it. Her son was standing before the judge. His head was bent and he looked all alone in the world. The judge was speaking. She ran down the aisle.

"Son! Son! Your mother's here. I'm here son!"

The judge was saying,

"And it's only because you have no mother or father that I'm going to give you probation instead of five years. You committed a serious . . . what did that woman say?"

She stopped and tried to tiptoe out backwards. She bumped smack into the bailiff. He was smiling.

"She said she's his mother, your honor."

THE QUESTION
AUGUST 29, 1960

"And when was the last time you saw a man under your bed, madam?"

"Well, doctor, it was last night. I had taken off my . . . well, I was ready for bed, and I saw or rather I heard this voice under my bed. I heard it so clear. It said . . . 'Can I?' That's all it said doctor. Just those two words, 'Can I?' Well, naturally I didn't know what to say, so I . . . well, I . . ."

"What did you say, madam?"

"Well, I said . . . Now doctor, I don't think you are really trying to treat me by asking me such irrelevant questions. I don't see why I should pay a psychologist good money just to have him ask me what I said to a man who was under my bed. I want you to stop these awful headaches. That's why my doctor sent me to you. He said that you could stop these headaches. I don't know how we got on this topic anyway . . ."

"What did you say to the man when he asked you if . . . well, when he said, 'Can I?'"

"Well, I don't think that's any of your business, doctor."

She quit seeing that doctor after that.

TIME ALONE
SEPTEMBER 1, 1960

"I am sorry; I'm not going to waste anymore of my time sitting around with them winoes, and lollygagging and all that jive. I'm going to make something out of my life. I'm not eighty years old. I've got a few years left . . . I'm sure of that."

The doctors walked over where he lay. One moved toward his chart. The other whispered him away from it, saying there was no need to look at it, that the old man would be dead by evening anyway, and that to fool around with a chart was just plain nonsense. The other doctor agreed. They looked at the patient. He was moving his lips. Once it sounded like he was saying something about . . . "years left."

THE LAST TIME
SEPTEMBER 5, 1960

I got to stop messing with that girl. She's going out of her skull. Anytime I wake up and see her standing over me with a knife in her hand crying I know I'm supposed to let up on her. I think I'll get home early today. I'm not going nowhere—straight home. That's just what I'm going to do. I mean like if it bugs her that much for me to be away why I'll just make it on in.

I can't stand it. He's not coming home today. I know it. I know he doesn't love me anymore. Why should I lie to myself about it? I mean if he wants to stay away, why don't I let him? But why didn't he do this before I started to love him so? How can I say goodbye now? But how can I take this, this indignity? What am I going to do? Life doesn't mean a thing to me anymore. Maybe I'd be better off dead. Maybe he'll think about me then . . . maybe he'll know how much I loved him. I don't care if I live or die. I don't want to go on this way, but I don't want to die. But I can't keep letting him hurt me.

Death is such an easy way out. But I can't suffer anymore. I . . . I just can't. If he's late today . . . I'm going to kill myself. There's no other way . . . no other way out.

Well, it's time to go home. Boy, five o'clock sure got here quick. I'm going straight home. I don't want any stuff out of that crazy woman.

"Hey, Daddy, let's have a little taste before you make it in."

"Naw, man, I'm going to swoop right now."

"Aww, you scared the old lady's gon' whup you or something. Ain't you a man?"

"Okay, just one, but after that . . ."

THE TIP
SEPTEMBER 6, 1960

"Who is this? Who's calling? Uh madam can you hold the wire a minute?"

"No, I can't hold the wire. I can't give you my name. You just go where I told you to. You'll find the guy who killed Robert Lee Taylor. I don't mean it. Just forget about what I said. No, don't forget about what I said. He did me wrong, now he got to pay. You go up there, you'll find him with a . . . a woman."

She clicked up the phone. She went home.

"Hi, Baby."

"What? . . . Buddy! What you doing here?"

"I was at Norma Jean's house. I picked up my records and things. I told her to forget it. Baby, I know I played you for a fool, but . . . but I want to come back. I told her I love you, and I . . . I want you to marry me."

Silence. Then,

"Buddy, how long does it take for the police to trace a telephone call?"

"Only a few minutes, why?"

A siren sounded outside, another sounded, and another. Buddy ran to the window. Red lights were flashing atop black cars. Men in plain-clothes were rushing out of the cars into the hallway and up the stairs.

Buddy looked at Delores. She looked at him. Buddy started to say something but he couldn't.

She started to say something, but she couldn't. Somebody knocked at the door . . .

THE ERRAND
SEPTEMBER 7, 1960

"Bye daddy."
"Bye baby . . . you look after mommy."
"And the new little baby too?"
"Yes, the new little baby too, I'm just going to the store for some milk so I won't be long, hear?"
"Okay daddy."
He kissed his wife, and the new little baby; and his big five year old daughter. He walked to the corner store four blocks away. He bumped into a policeman. He kept walking.
"Hey, aren't you going to say excuse me?"
"Oh, 'scuse me."
"You did that on purpose, didn't you?"
"No sir, I didn't."
"Come here, you must be one of those Egyptian Cobras."[34]
He came. The policeman hit him.
"Get up!"
The policeman hit him again. He fell. The policeman kicked him. He got up. The policeman drew back to hit him again. He snatched the policeman's gun from his holster. He was crying. He aimed and pulled the trigger. The policeman fell. A lady came up. She looked at the dead policeman. She looked at him. She screamed. A crowd came. Somebody grabbed him and held him.

FUGUE
SEPTEMBER 8, 1960

Walking along the high edge of a glass wall thin as a window's pane. Blowing wind down the cloud holes, and across the sun fingers and

---

34. The Egyptian Cobras were a street gang formed on Chicago's west side in 1954. Members later changed their name to the Mickey Cobras.

into the eyes, and ears. Screaming GLORY, GLORY TO GOD IN THE HIGHEST. At Madison and State and seeing inside the shirt pockets and size B cups the whirl and muck of green nights and loud music calling the soldiers from Africa to Mississippi to whip the money changers from the temples, and to spread yellow and warmth and joy over the shame of last night's lusting and ocean rocking dreaming and deepening blood and life's heartbeat inside the FIRST PLACE. Walking and handing to hands the leaflets shouting SINNER REPENT! Waiting for the lashes of the knife snow. Lying on the desert in the mind for the sun's eatings, and calling to the picture of the old dark lady on the mantle for another chance to love. And knowing that sleep takes and gives not, and knowing that it is this LAST SLEEP that is really what screams down from the hills, whistling in the screaming; this and the great double-bladed stereophonic, cinematic popcorn and candy and red suited usher's final blow.

D. O. A.
SEPTEMBER 13, 1960

"I can't help it. I'm going to see her. Lay low. How can I lay low when I love her so? Oh God, tell me what to do! I know I'm wrong but..."

And at her house:

"Charles, why are you carrying that gun around the house? I told you that I'm not seeing Harvey anymore. I...told him that I was...well, through. Isn't that what I told you I said?"

"Yes that's what you told me, but I don't believe you. Don't you think I hear you calling his name in your sleep? Don't you realize you've called me Harvey even when we've been talking? Don't you know I've seen you staring out of the car into space when I've taken you for rides? You are still in love with that filthy double crosser, and I swear I'm going to kill him if he comes here tonight."

"Is that why you stayed home from work?"

"And that's why I don't want you to make any phone calls. I don't want anybody to warn him. I'll see if you're really through with him or not. And for his sake you'd better be. I'll see you dead in hell and him too, before I let him have you."

It was then that there was the sound of a key in the door and the door opened slowly at first and then quickly, and a man said,

"Honey? ..."

STRANGE PARTY
SEPTEMBER 14, 1960

So she was talking to me, yes I know that, but don't you think I know what she was really thinking? Oh, I saw that look in her eyes, and I watched her lean toward me when she talked. Oh she's a sly one but I know her, and I'll meet her someday when we are alone and I'll ... oh oh, here she comes. Now look at her. Smiling.

"Oh yes. I do. Do you? Oh that's nice. No, no I never have. Really? Ha, ha, ha, ha. Well, I'd say yes, actually though, I don't think many people would agree with me. You do? Really? Well, isn't that a coincidence. How did you come to think like that? Really? You did? Well, I'll be darned. Excuse you? Why certainly. 'Bye."

Ohhh how slick can you be. Trying to whip the game on me. I fooled her; she thought I was going to say it. Didn't she? But she doesn't move me. Not one little bit. Her green eyes, and that tight dress, and those lips saying things to me. Oh I know her kind, but she'll never get me. I ... oh she's coming back ...

"What? Oh yes. Why certainly. Sure, I'd be glad to. Oh, I didn't think you meant. I just said that I would be glad to ... No I didn't ask you to ... well if that's the way you ... what? Okay then, goodbye!"

Why that dirty ...

1903456, CLARKSDALE, MISS.
SEPTEMBER 19, 1960

"Who sent you here to spy on us?"

"My name is John Richards, sir. My serial number is 1903456."

"Why would you, of all people undertake an assignment like this? What have they done for you? Who do you think you are helping by engaging in such a mission as this?"

"My name is John Richards, sir. My serial number is 1903456."

"Do you realize that you will be tortured until you talk? Don't you realize that we are trying to help you? You're a fool. Come, tell me. What were your orders?"

"My name is John Richards, sir. My serial number is 1903456."

"And what was Emmett Till's serial number? Or Mack Charles Parker's? Don't you think we know about such things? Are you going to remain silent in spite of . . . of everything?"

"My name is John Richards, sir. My serial number is 1903456."

"Shoot him!"

THE RED HANDLE
SEPTEMBER 20, 1960

Sgt. Taylor kicked Major Hollis in the stomach. The Major opened his mouth but no sound came out. He grabbed Taylor's leg and pulled him to the floor. He started to run back to the set of controls, and he reached for the red painted handle, but couldn't touch it before Taylor dived into his back and chopped two judo blows at the back of his neck.

Hollis shifted his weight at the last second, causing the blows to land on his shoulder. He grabbed Taylor's hand and bit it. Taylor cried out and swung hard with his other hand. Hollis fell backwards. As he fell his hand touch the leg of a chair, he swung the chair in front of him just as Taylor dived at him. Taylor smashed against the edges of the chair.

He grunted and toppled to his side. Hollis scrambled to the red knob again. Taylor threw the chair at Hollis and missed, but it distracted Hollis enough to allow Taylor time to grab his wrist . . . to prevent the crazed man from pulling the red-handled switch under which was a sign that read HYDROGEN BOMB No. 1.

Hollis and Taylor wrestled and fought and wrestled and fought and wrestled and fought . . .

THE HIPPIES
SEPTEMBER 21, 1960

"Hey man! What are you doing down here?"

"Well I'll be . . . How did you make it over here? Look, there's Bobo over there. See the guy in the fatigues and the automatic rifle . . . and the shades?"

"Whaaat? He's still as hip as ever. Hey Bobo! What you doing in the Congo baby? I thought you'd be on the set hittin' on all the young foxes."

"Heey, Skeeter! Jim, I thought I was the only one to get that old time Spanish Civil War itch.[35] What's happening? Anybody else here?"

"I haven't seen anybody else. Dig, look at all these funny lookin' studs around here. Like that long lanky cat in the corner. He'd give Wilt the Stilt[36] a run for his bread."

"Dig, Skeeter. That cat's from Kenya. He's a Kikuyu. I hear he's a fightin' somitch. He was in Algeria with the rebels and now he's over here."

"Attention!"

Everybody stood. The officer looked like a real bad Chicago policeman. But his English was something else.

"Gentlemen, I am exceedingly happy to see so many volunteers from the countries of the world. Remain standing, Premier Lumumba[37] is coming to address you."

The three Chicago hippies were the straightest standing studs in the whole barracks.

THE LEADER
SEPTEMBER 22, 1960

And so you've found out. Well, perhaps it's time. Look around you . . . wait, wait; put the gun away for a minute. I know I must die. It comes as no surprise. I'm prepared for it. Put the gun away for a minute.

Now, that's better. Now look around you. See that old man dragging that cotton sack? See his eyes? Watch him as he passes us. Watch the look he gives you. Ah! See it? See! Was there fear in his eyes? Didn't you note a kind of smile? Let me tell you, sheriff; he knows that you've lost.

Here, look at the young boy beside you. See it there? And there!

---

35. During the Spanish Civil War (1936-39), many Americans volunteered to fight for the leftist Republicans.

36. Basketball legend Wilt Chamberlain.

37. Patrice Lumumba, first prime minister of the Republic of the Congo, who was assassinated in January 1961.

Look over there, those young girls playing on the sidewalk. Did you notice that they did not move when that white couple went by? Oh, I know all about the "accidental" death of the last Leader down here. I've been briefed. I'm ready. My work...my work, mind you, is over down here. Shoot, Sheriff...I'm ready.

NITTY GRITTY
SEPTEMBER 27, 1960

It was the first day of school. The teacher walked into the room. A kind of tension between this dark haired white woman and the Negro students flared up the minute she walked in.

Somebody coughed. Everybody laughed.

Somebody else imitated Ray Charles, saying, "W'now she's alright shesalright!"

Everybody laughed again. The teacher rapped on the desk for silence. Nothing happened. She sat prim and proper. And she was properly outraged. She remembered the time at Austin and Senn and how when they'd found out about her husband, they'd found some way to get her out of those schools. Still, nine years of marriage to a Negro and life in the ghetto had taught her how to deal with "her people." Now she was just a white woman. She knew something else was needed to make them see her as a human being. She looked around the room and glanced at the door, and said quietly and firmly,

"Now I'm getting tired of this three-six-nine. Shut up!"

Everybody was cool from then on.

THE TEACHER
SEPTEMBER 28, 1960

"Now Miss Warren, I'm helping you with this anthropology course because you seem to be interested in knowing more about mankind, and because you intend to be a teacher. I hope you will feel free to discuss this course with me after class, at coffee or dinner or...well, whenever and wherever you wish. I say again I'm very interested in students who wish to explore the field of anthropology. You've got quite a lot of talent for this sort of thing, and I believe that if you apply yourself, you'll pass this course with ease.

I'm going to give you my home phone number so that if you should have any question . . . any question at all about the extended family, or Puberty Ritual you can feel free to call me. Okay? Okay! Oh, yes, if a woman should answer . . . hang up."

EASTERN MOUTH
SEPTEMBER 29, 1960

The trap was set, there was no other place for him to run. He'd broken up Garfield Boulevard and under the "L" at Fifty-Fifth Street, and over to Fifty-Fifth Place, and toward South Parkway. They'd blocked off Prairie at Fifty-Fifth Place and they'd blocked off Sixty-Sixth Street under the "L" and at South Parkway and Prairie. They were right on his heels, so he couldn't backtrack onto Fifty-Fifth Street again. There was only one place for him to go and that was east of South Parkway. They set up a front line of detectives and policemen, all armed with submachine guns and shotguns, on both sides of the eastern mouth of Fifty-Fifth Place. There was no doubt about what they intended to do . . . he'd killed a policeman.

Now they waited. It got dark. He was not in sight, but they waited anyway. Finally, a skinny figure climbed out of a basement in the parking lot at Fifty-Fifth Place. He looked about from left to right, from North to South. He saw a policeman go by the western end of Fifty-Fifth Place. He thought about heading south under the "L," but he changed his mind. There was only one way to go, and that was toward the Park, toward South Parkway . . . to the eastern mouth of Fifty-Fifth Place. He took a deep breath, hitched up his pants, glanced around just once more and started running, as fast as he could, toward . . .

THE ACCIDENT
OCTOBER 4, 1960

She lived on Sixty-Seventh. And he lived on Forty-Seventh.

"Well, Mary, if that's the way you feel about it. You just don't have to sit here and argue with me. I can't be taking you out every time you feel like it. I work—every day. And I'm tired. If you want to go out— like go. You know? I mean . . . you know?"

"Byeeeee."

And at Forty-Seventh:

"Talk to you? About what? Robert, I've got these kids to fight with all day. I mean talk to you about what? Life? What about life? I'm in life. Why talk about it? Where you going? Robert? Robert?"

Two figures moved northward and southward. At Fifty-Fifth and South Parkway a woman stepped out of a jitney. She crossed the street, heading toward Washington Park. Another jitney pulled up just as she reached the other side. A man got out. He glanced up as he stepped out. The woman glanced down. He didn't smile. She didn't smile. He walked toward her. She dropped her purse; things fell out of it. He stooped to help her . . .

EPISTROPHY
OCTOBER 5, 1960

Five shots blasted at him. The woman was still screaming. He climbed the fire escape. Someone was running behind him. He leaped from the fire escape to a nearby porch. Another shot. The splinters from the brick wall where the bullet had hit splattered against his face. He blinked his eyes and kept running. He could still hear the woman screaming. He dove head first into a window from the porch. He broke through the house, found the front door and crashed down the stairs. People came to see what had happened, but he was out of the front door by then, and onto the street and in the crowd that gathered to see what was going on. He saw his car across the street. He walked to it, got in it and drove home.

"Honey, is that you?"

"Yes dear."

"Have a hard day at the office, honey?"

He pecked her on the cheek and went to the paper in the living room. Bach was on the FM.

"Yes dear, a very hard day."

THE FRIEND
OCTOBER 6, 1960

"Man, I'm not signifying, but if anybody talked about my mother the way that cat talked about yours. I mean playing is playing, but he was playing the dozens, Jim."

"What did he say?"

"Well, I ain't in it. I was just in the crowd when he was talking. I don't want to agitate or nothing like that. You know!"

"Where is he?"

"He's right downstairs. Come on. I'll show you where he is."

"What did he say?"

"Wait a minute! Look! There he is! Hey, Martin! Hey Martin! Hold it a minute, Smitty wants to talk you! Come on Smitty, he's waiting."

"Hi, Smitty."

"What did you say about my mother, Martin?"

"Your mother? Who said I said . . . where's Lloyd? Where'd he go?"

"Why he was here just a min . . . Lloyd? Lloyd!"

"Dig, Jim, that cat told me that you said . . ."

"And he told me YOU said . . ."

PURSUIT
OCTOBER 13, 1960

She walked to him. She kissed and leaned into him, arms loose around his neck. Her breath smelled like fresh milk. He felt what he'd been feeling just a moment ago go away when she did that. The surge was coming from without him now. At first it had come from within. Something seemed short-circuited. He wanted to stop, but he'd started it. Had played with her hair, and had looked at her—calling things from deep inside her, calling them up and out, and to him. He'd done that, yes he had. And now that she was upon him—there as he'd insisted with his eyes that she be—now that she WAS there. HE DIDN'T WANT HER.

"What . . . what's the matter, honey?"

"I don't know."

"You don't know."

"I don't know."
She moved away.
"Oh."

THE MORTAL[38]
OCTOBER 24, 1960

"Hey, brother Lou! What's happenin'?"
Louis turned, saw and waved. He walked into a cafeteria and sat at the counter.
"Whatcha want, baby?"
"Coffee."
Her tone, like the other guy's—a Fifty-Eighth Street junkie—was familiar, too much so. He'd arrested her once on Sixty-Third Street. She'd been afraid of him ever since; had spoken to him only when he caught her eye; had hurried by when he neared. Now she called him baby. He drank his coffee and went to the streets again.
"Hey, what happened Officer Lou, baby?"
It was another junkie. This one would have run from him before the story appeared in the paper: COP FIRED!
Somebody bumped into him, looked at him, turned the mouth corners down and sneered.
"Watch where you walking, you jive . . ."
For the first time in five years he was a mortal again. It was an odd feeling.

THE FIFTH NIGHT
OCTOBER 25, 1960

Sometime after two in the morning, he woke from a drowning sleep and the mossy greenish blue from the new streetlight outside his room pulled from the room's shade such off-the-wall objects as the upper half of his double edge razor on the dresser and part of the buckle of the belt upon his pants which lay on the floor at the side of the bed.
An airplane behind the clouds' black blanket Gaahhhhhhhhhed

---

38. Unsigned.

its way to the Midway airfield. A female cat downstairs moaned, and pleaded, and whined and suddenly stopped.

He thought about her.

He got up and went to the window, and looked down. No one was on the street. Yet, he knew that somewhere SHE was on the street. He went to the dresser and felt for his forty-five. He put it on the side of the bed. He sat on the side of the bed. He pulled his pants on and tucked in his shirttail and slipped into his coat and put the gun in the pocket. There is no other way. I must. If I can't have her . . . He walked to the street.

He wondered how it would feel to be strapped in an electric chair.

QUO VADIS
OCTOBER 26, 1960

It was downhill that they were running. There were clouds under their feet and sweet new-cut grass rushed down their throats. They held hands and they looked into each other's eyes. They kissed and they laughed. They fell to the softness of the soft cloud ground, and they lay there looking up at the trees and watching the blue on the edges of riverside blooming of bush.

She kissed him and he kissed her and they got up and ran some more. There was no one near and the sounds were those of low chirping birds and crickets in scores.

Above them, past all hearing and knowing, were voices of humans.

"Why did they do it?"

"Look they're floating to the surface."

"Oh, her arms are around him."

"And his are around her."

"Oh, the poor young things. The poor young things."

LIKE IT IS
OCTOBER 27, 1960

George tipped behind Little Boo and poked his finger in his ribs. Little Boo turned quickly and made a fake judo move and the two boys laughed and put their arms around each other and walked down Calumet toward Fifty-Seventh.

"Detective George Day! Step into the office!

"Detective Day, I know this is a nasty assignment, but you know this man Little Boo or Boo or whatever it is. He has killed two people. He must be caught. And you're the only one who knows his haunts, habits and well . . . I understand you were childhood friends."

Down Calumet again to Fifty-Seventh Street. The kitchenette where Linette still lived. Where she still loved him.

"Linette? This is George . . . George Day."

Footscuffles.

"Okay Little Boo, man. Come on out. This is George, man. Listen, I'll cop for you. I know what it can do to a . . ."

Three shots through the door. The Chief of Detectives took over.

"Okay men, break in. Detective Day, you come back here with me!"

Sawed-off shotguns, tear gas, automatics, rifles, fire, smoke, cracking wood, screams, feet running, more firing, a thud, a moan, more firing and silence . . . Little Boo was gone . . . and . . . well . . .

CIRCLE[39]
NOVEMBER 3, 1960

"But Tom, why won't you see me again? I don't want to beg you, but . . . okay Tom; if that's the way you feel about it. Goodbye Tom."

"Louise, this is Tom. I know. I know I called you yesterday. Yeah, yeah I know what your answer is, but Louise . . . please Louise. Let me see you. Just this once . . . Okay Louise. Okay . . . See yuh."

"Larry? This . . . this is Louise. I, uh, waited for you to call me like you said you would, Larry listen . . . Aww Larry, Larry, I'm sorry . . . I—'bye Larry."

"Pearl this is Larry. I've got a couple of tickets to . . . busy? Don't bother you anymore. Pearl this is Larry, I love . . . Pearl? Pearl! Goodbye Pearl."

Circle you go round and round
Yet will not stop where happiness is found.
You just go round and round.

---

39. Unsigned.

AFTERWORD[1]

BY NILE LANSANA

Frank London Brown's care for his craft and prolific storytelling range is extremely inspiring to me. The discipline in his writing practice of nearly creating a story every other day for a year shows how dearly he held this artistry. I wanted to channel that precision in my own work. However, I recognized that attempting to encapsulate the plethora of stories within *This Is Life* into one piece was like trying to fit an elephant into a briefcase. I chose to focus on "Stolen Thrill" and "Circle," two stories that moved my spirit deeply. Brown cherished and carefully examined the nuances of life with an open mind and a heart ablaze. I, too, want to live and create with a heart ablaze and an ever-expanding mind. I'm grateful to lend my gifts to this creative lineage in which Brown is a unsung titan.

STOLEN THRILL

Dawry sits on the red plush couch, laptop linked up to our apartment television, playing his favorite movie featuring his melodic mind & antsy hands making songs on Logic Pro.

    I wrestle with Italian homework on Canvas, a college
    student's favorite nemesis, at our living room desk.
Fiddling with audio clips trying to fit the puzzle into hymn, Dawry shapeshifts samples and sound bites into boom-bap symphony.

    Wrapping up my final sentence about being an AC Milan
    fan in il congiuntivo,

---

1. I wanted to see how Brown's stories might speak to later generations of Black writers. After seeing Nile Lansana perform some of his poems at a Juneteenth celebration in 2022, I asked him to respond to these stories in whatever way he chose. – Ed.

I click "Submit" with gusto and close my laptop.
Letting Logic rest to pull up Spotify, we sigh out exhaustion in
unison, inhale the ecstatic energy of New Music Friday.
Kenny Mason's "Partments" rings in our ritual of scorching
sixteens, moscato sips, and feverish head nods.
With a hook so infectious we put it on repeat, I rap with my brother
who know I got his back, who don't gotta tell me he got my back.
Unknown when we will return to our favorite club around
the corner or a house party's heat, jumping around our living
room to fresh tunes is the most turnt up time of our week.
Isolation could keep our spirits stone cold, murder & disease could
keep our hearts shattered, but these thrills we turn to can't be stolen.
This energy we cultivate carries us to ecstasy, far from
assignment and assailant.

CIRCLE

If I must go, let litanies of love leave me behind
Let souls fortify at the sight of my psalms
Grins & tears & laughs galore as your life
Grows richer by inheriting my tales
Currency you never have to release
Fairytales penned by a South Side sun

Fairytales penned by a South Side sun
Currency you never have to release
By inheriting my tales, your life grows
Richer, grins & tears & laughs galore
Let souls fortify at the sight of my psalms
If I must go, let litanies of love leave me behind

Revolved my life around what lifts my spirit
So I give life past my limp bones, eternal healing

BIOS

FRANK LONDON BROWN

Frank London Brown (1927-1962) was a novelist, union organizer, journalist, singer, father, and husband. Born in Kansas City, Missouri, Brown moved at the age of 12 with his family to Chicago. He attended DuSable High School and Roosevelt University, and he received his Master's degree from the University of Chicago, where he worked toward a Ph.D. in the Committee on Social Thought. As a journalist, he wrote for numerous newspapers and journals, including the *Chicago Sun-Times*, *Ebony*, the *Chicago Tribune*, *Negro Digest*, and the *Chicago Defender*. It was at the *Defender* that he gained nationwide recognition through his coverage of the murder of Emmett Till in Mississippi. Fervently progressive, Brown also worked as a union organizer and was active in the Civil Rights Movement. A major voice in Chicago's Black Renaissance, he made his literary reputation with the 1959 publication of his semi-autobiographical first novel, *Trumbull Park*, which remains the best literary portrait of Northern segregation. His death in 1962 cut short what would have been a stellar literary career, a fact underscored by his posthumously published second novel, *The Myth Maker*, in 1969.

DEBRA E. BROWN-THOMPSON

Debra E. Brown-Thompson, CEO of The Learnatory, empowers individuals to exceed expectations. Her program, "Envision Success," develops civically-engaged citizens who embrace disruption for transformation. She cultivates emotionally intelligent next-gen leaders who navigate paradoxes, strengthening businesses and communities. She's a proud mother of three.

SANDRA JACKSON-OPOKU

Sandra Jackson-Opoku is author of the award-winning novel *The River Where Blood Is Born* (1997) and the Essence Magazine Bestseller *Hot Johnny (and the Women Who Loved Him)* (2001). She also coedited the anthology *Revise the Psalm: Work Celebrating the Writing of Gwendolyn Brooks* (2017). Her fiction, nonfiction, and dramatic works are widely published and produced. She has won a National Endowment for the Arts Fellowship, the American Library Association Black Caucus Award, a City of Chicago Esteemed Literary Artist Award, the Plentitudes Journal Fiction Prize, the Globe Soup Story Award, a Pushcart Prize nomination, the Circle of Confusion Writers Discovery Fellowship, and other awards. She presents literary readings, artist talks, and writing workshops throughout the country and around the world.

NILE LANSANA

Nile Lansana is an acclaimed interdisciplinary artist from the South Side of Chicago. His work is centered around revealing radical truths and amplifying marginalized voices and narratives through a lens of Black imagination and visionary intention. He was nominated for the inaugural Chicago Poet Laureate position. A graduate of the University of Wisconsin-Madison, he directed and premiered his first documentary *We the Vision* in March 2022. He's an award-winning poet and performer who's graced stages across the country, including Lollapalooza and the Kennedy Center. He holds fellowships from the Rebuild Foundation and Obsidian Foundation. He is a proud uncle and the oldest of four Black boys. IG: @nilesupasuit

REBECCA ZORACH

Rebecca Zorach is the Mary Jane Crowe Professor in Art and Art History at Northwestern University. She curated the exhibition *The Time is Now: Art Worlds of Chicago's South Side 1960–1980* at the

Smart Museum of Art in 2018. Her books include *Blood, Milk, Ink, Gold: Abundance and Excess in the French Renaissance* (2005), *Gold: Nature and Culture* (with Michael W. Phillips Jr., 2016), and *Art for People's Sake: Artists and Community in Black Chicago 1965–1975* (2019).